NORTHLINE

by the same author

THE MOTEL LIFE

NORTHLINE

a novel

WILLY VLAUTIN

faber and faber

First published in 2008
by Faber and Faber Limited
3 Queen Square London WC1N 3AU

Typeset by Faber and Faber Limited
Printed in England by Mackays of Chatham, plc

The right of Willy Vlautin to be identified as author of this work
has been asserted in accordance with Section 77 of the Copyright,
Designs and Patents Act 1988

A CIP record for this book
is available from the British Library

ISBN 978–0–571–23570–4

2 4 6 8 10 9 7 5 3 1

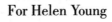

For Helen Young

CIRCUS CIRCUS

They were above them, the circus people, in costumes, swinging from ropes. A net was below and a small band played lifelessly in the corner, in near darkness. Colored spotlights followed the performers and an announcer introduced them and told the gathering crowd what was to come.

Jimmy Bodie stood watching, drinking a beer while the girl sat near the video games, drunk. She was in her early twenties, an average-looking girl, thin with black hair and blue eyes.

'I think Warren and Nan got a room,' he said when the show ended.

'They did?' she said and stood. 'That's what she said she wanted for her birthday.'

'I guess she got it.'

'Was it a good show?'

'They're all the same,' he said.

'I can't believe they don't get scared all the way up there.'

'It's practice,' he said and finished the bottle. 'Those fuckers probably practice all day long. Let's go, I need another.'

'I guess I could have another, too,' the girl said and they began walking.

'You're done for tonight.'

'I'm not that drunk,' she said.

'You can barely walk right. Anyway, you've passed out at the last four parties we've been to. Everyone thinks you're a drunk.'

'I wasn't that drunk at all those parties. Maybe one or two, but not all.'

They took an escalator down to the casino's main floor. Jimmy went to the bar and ordered two beers. He gave one to the girl.

'Just don't pass out on me tonight,' he told her.

'I won't,' she said, but she knew it was coming. She tried to count the beers she'd had, but couldn't.

'Did I tell you I used to work here?'

'I'm not sure. I knew you worked at a few places but . . .'

'I was a maintenance man. Me and this old guy, Turquoise. He was named that when he was a Marine. He always wore a turquoise ring that belonged to his sister who got cancer or something horrible like that. Maybe MS. I don't know. I never even knew his real name, but I guess that doesn't matter. He was a good guy, an old timer. He'd been around the casinos forever. He hated Mexicans – man, I never saw a guy that hated spicks as much as that guy. He wouldn't even eat Mexican food, not even Taco Bell. He and I used to walk back to the kitchen of this fancy restaurant upstairs, he knew the head cook, they were friends, so he would set us up with steaks and shrimp every Wednesday night. Huge steaks, T-bones. They had a table in the back for employees. We'd just sit there and eat and eat. He'd keep bringing us out all this food. We'd be on the clock and he'd be telling me about being in the Marines in Korea, all kinds of crazy shit. Blowing up villages, killing people, friends of his who got their heads blown off.'

'I don't think you've mentioned him before,' she said.

'I'll show you something,' he told her and took her hand and they began to walk. 'I'll never work in the casinos again. They treat you like shit, they don't give a fuck if you come or go. The management doesn't give a fuck because they know you're going to quit and they know someone else will take your job the next day. I stayed here a couple years then Turquoise retired. He was gonna move to Bullhead City with his wife. He was through with it. Tired of Vegas, tired of training people. We used to go through them. He'd done maybe fifteen years with Circus Circus, and they didn't give him shit. Not a thanks or nothing, and that guy could fix anything. When he quit, I took his job, but it wasn't any fun without him. I got sick of it and went back to work at Bob's shop.

'Anyway,' he said and stopped. 'See that door?' He pointed to a hallway. 'It's not marked or anything, but it's an executive bathroom. I used to take this cocktail waitress in there.'

'I don't want to hear what you did in there with someone else,' the girl said. She finished her beer. She was beginning to have trouble standing. Her words came to her slowly, stumbling out. She didn't want to go in there.

'I'm with you now. Don't worry. But I used to go with this girl, and she and me we've done it in every dump from here to old town. From the MGM to the Plaza, end to end and everything in between.'

'Who?'

'You don't know her. She might not even be in town anymore.'

'I told you I don't like to hear about it.'

'Don't worry,' he said and put his hand around her waist.

He led her towards the bathroom. The girl started to get the spins. All the lights and slot machines, and the people everywhere. She looked at an old man in a wheelchair playing video keno. He was missing both legs, cut off just below his knees. He wore an old brown western shirt, a cowboy hat, his face was red from booze and gray with stubble.

Jimmy opened the door to the bathroom and led her inside.

'What we gonna do in here?' the girl asked and tried to smile.

'What do you think?'

'What if we get caught?'

A set of fluorescent lights hung from overhead. The walls were pale white. There was a urinal, two sinks, and two stalls. Jimmy took the girl's hand and led her into the handicap stall and kissed her. He ran his hand through her black hair and kissed her neck. He grabbed her shirt and pulled it over her head. He unconnected her bra and threw it in the corner.

'I don't want to get all the way naked. What if someone comes in?'

'No one will come in.' He dropped to his knees. 'If someone does, we'll just have to be quiet is all.' He took off her black leather shoes, unbuttoned her skirt, and pulled it down to her ankles.

'If we're gonna do this, I need another drink.'

He handed her the beer he'd set on the tile floor.

She took a long drink and finished it.

He kissed her legs. He moved his hands to her thin black underwear, and ripped them from her and threw them on the floor.

'Jesus,' she said, 'are you gonna buy me some new ones?'

'As long as they're black and G-strings.' He began kissing between her legs.

'They're uncomfortable.'

'I don't mind,' he said.

'You wouldn't,' she said and ran her hands through his hair. She wanted it to feel good, but she was drunk. It became difficult just standing. She took a hold of the rails. After a time he stood up. He unbuttoned his pants.

'You all right?'

'I think I am.'

He kissed her, then turned her around, and she leaned over the toilet, with her arms stretched out and holding onto the seat.

'Are you wearing a rubber?' she asked but she knew it didn't matter any longer.

'No,' he said. 'I'm not gonna anymore, either. I want you and me to have a kid.'

'I'm only twenty-two.'

'I don't want to talk about that right now. I hate talking when I'm fucking, you know that.'

He moved inside her. He ran his hands over her back, over her tattoos. He put his fingers on the small of her back where there was a silver-dollar-sized black swastika. Just above it to the left was a tattoo of the World Church of the Creator emblem. A circle with a large W inside it. He kept moving inside her. She tried to hold on, to keep standing, but she was beginning to black out. He wouldn't stop. She tried to focus on the stainless steel pipe that was connected to the toilet, tried to read the words stamped into it.

When she fell, her head hit the metal pipe and cut a half inch line above her left eye, just above the eye lid. Blood ran down her face as she lay naked on the floor.

He pulled up his pants then bent down and moved her so she was sitting up. Blood leaked down her face. He tried to stop it with toilet paper.

'Wake up,' he said and shook her. He wasn't sure what to do. He wanted to leave her there to teach her a lesson. He was ashamed of her, of the way she drank, the way she would just fall apart. He sat down next to her but his temper grew, and then he felt a wetness.

He looked down and she was urinating. He stood up and yelled at her again.

'Get up,' he said over and over and his voice grew louder. But she didn't move and he knew he'd have to dress her and carry her out.

He still knew people that worked there. He thought of everyone looking at him, sneering at him, making comments about him and his girlfriend. Maybe security would stop him, maybe the police would come.

He looked at her, at the blood again leaking, dripping from the cut. He saw the small pool of urine around her, and he kicked her. Just once, but as hard as he could, with his steel-toed boots. Kicked her in the leg, above the knee. Still she didn't move, so he reached down for her clothes and began to dress her.

THE BASEMENT

She woke the next morning in his apartment. It was a studio that had been built in the basement of an old house. It had concrete floors, an unfinished ceiling, and cinder block walls painted white. She could hear the TV in the background. It was still early, just past sunrise, and light was beginning to hit the small window above the bed. She could hear him doing push ups on the floor and could smell coffee brewing. Her head hurt and she could barely sit up she was so sore.

'What happened?' she asked when he stood up. He was shirtless, his chest and arms bare, no tattoos. He wore blue jeans and black boots. Sweat dripped from his face.

'You passed out in the bathroom at Circus Circus. You fell down and hit your head on the toilet. I don't think you need stitches, but maybe you should check with a doctor. Maybe you have a concussion. I taped it the best I could. I tried to keep you awake but there wasn't a chance of that. You remember anything?'

'Not really,' she said and smiled nervously.

'I had to dress you after you pissed all over yourself. I had to carry you out the door. Security stopped me. Everyone was standing around, looking at me, looking at you. I had to explain it to them. They wanted to arrest me. They wanted to call the police, but I talked them out of it.'

She got off the bed and stood naked. She looked at her leg and saw the dark bruise just above the knee. She limped into the bathroom.

When she came out he was frying eggs in a pan with bacon.

'I'm gonna go down to the shop. I don't feel like being around you today.'

'I'm sorry,' the girl said and got back in bed. 'I really am.' She sat up with her back against the wall and covered herself with a blanket.

'I don't know what happened.'

He walked over to her and stood in front of her.

'You used to be all right.'

'I know.'

'I don't see how you can do that to yourself. You should be in AA. At least you'd have respect for yourself then.'

'I know,' she said and tried to look at him.

'I'm tired of you embarrassing me, embarrassing yourself. And then you apologize. You apologize over and over but it's still the same old fucking thing.'

'Did you sleep last night?' she asked.

'I don't know the last time I slept. But I'm not the one that passed out in Circus Circus.'

There was an American flag hanging by the door, and a lamp made from a fender off a 1946 Ford coupé. There was a couch and a table with books about cars, mechanic books, books on guns and self defense, books on tattoos, books on immigration, US history books. There was a framed picture of his mom and dad that hung over the TV, which was sitting on a beat-up stereo cabinet. He had a computer on a metal desk, and a corkboard behind it full of notes and articles he had found. There were records on the floor. Hank Williams, Johnny Cash, David Alan Coe, Buck Owens, Chet Atkins. Hundreds of country and rockabilly records.

He stood at the foot of the bed staring at her, then went to the stove, took the pan from the burner, and set it on a table that sat against the wall. He went to his dresser and took a pair of handcuffs from a drawer. He walked back to her, grabbed her left arm, and locked her wrist in the handcuff and locked the other side to the bed frame.

'This is what it's like being with you. Last night was like being handcuffed to a fucking bed. Imagine walking through Circus Circus with all the security and people watching, and then all the way to the car with people watching, and the whole time carrying that fucking bed. That's what it's like to be with you.'

He didn't say anything else, he just pulled the blanket off the bed. She lay there naked and began crying. He went to a cupboard, took a plate from it, dished his eggs and bacon onto it, but he couldn't eat. He left the plate full, poured himself a cup of coffee, and left.

THE VERDICT

It was ten hours before he came back. He stood in the doorway and took off his clothes. He was haggard and could barely talk. He came into the room, unlocked her, and collapsed onto the bed.

'I'm sorry,' he said and closed his eyes. He held her against him and fell asleep. She could smell the speed in his sweat and the alcohol on his breath. She waited for nearly an hour, until his breathing was steady and sure, before she got up. She then found her clothes, dressed, and left as quietly as she could.

It was past five p.m. when she made it to a main street and was able to catch a bus to her mother's house. When she got off at her stop she walked to a mini-mart and bought a half a pint of vodka and a large fountain 7UP. Outside on the sidewalk she sat down, poured out a third of the soda onto the street, and replaced it with vodka. The sun was beginning to set and the heat was letting up. She took a long drink. She stood up and looked at her reflection in the window of a parked car and tried to fix her hair and clean her face.

Her mother's house was in North Las Vegas. It was a two bedroom ranch house built in the 1960s and painted white with green trim, but the paint was now faded and cracking. There was a patch of grass in the front and a larger one at the back. Both were brown and dying. A carport with a green plastic roof ran alongside the house and wrapped around the back porch. As she walked up her street she could see her mom's 1987 burgundy Chevy Lumina parked underneath it.

The air conditioner was on inside and her mother sat on the couch drinking a can of beer, watching TV. The blinds were closed and the only light besides the television came from a lamp next to the couch.

'Hey,' the girl said and sat down across from her in a recliner.

'How was your day?' her mom asked and then coughed. She was dressed in a worn-out Chinese silk robe. She was forty-seven years old and thin, with black hair flecked with gray. Her teeth were brown and she'd had three pulled that year. She had the face of a woman who drank every day and forgot to eat when she did. She took a Marlboro from a pack on her lap and lit one.

'I dropped a tray with four plates on it this morning,' the girl said. 'I tripped and then dropped the order, then hit my face on a table. The food went flying everywhere. It was the most embarrassing thing. Everyone stopped. The whole restaurant just stopped and became silent. You've been there. You've seen how big it is. Can you tell if my face looks bad?'

The mother sat up, and the girl leaned over so her mom could see.

'You poor thing,' she said. 'It doesn't look too bad. But you should clean it out with hydrogen peroxide. I hated waitressing. Did someone trip you?'

'No, it was just me being me.'

'I've done worse, much worse.' Her mother sat back and looked at the TV. 'Look, here he is,' she said and coughed again. 'A Paul Newman marathon. I was gonna call you, but I couldn't find Jimmy's number. Will you write it down again and put it on the fridge? Anyway, it's Paul Newman, all night and all day. Your dream man's on a TNT Marathon. Paul Newman for twenty-four hours.'

'Really,' the girl said and tried to smile. 'I rented *The Verdict* again last week. That's what this one is. It's a good one.'

'It seems like it.'

'So you still like Paul Newman, too?'

'That's one thing I don't change on,' her mother said and laughed.

'Does it go on all night?'

'All night.'

'Do you mind if I stay here tonight?'

'Of course not.' She took a drink from her beer, finishing it, and set it on the coffee table.

'You just get off?'

'An hour ago. I'm supposed to go back on nights, but it's a nice break to live like a normal human being for once. How's the Plaza?'

'All right,' the girl said and took a drink from the soda.

'You should start dealing. It's not the best life, but the money's pretty good. At least you don't have to carry trays of food and bang your head into a table.'

'I've been thinking about it. I don't know. You need another?'

'I got one in the freezer. It should be cold enough by now.'

The girl went into the kitchen and took the beer from the freezer and set it on the counter. She opened the refrigerator and looked inside. It was bare except for condiments, a quart of milk, a head of wilted iceberg lettuce, a gallon jug of water, and a half empty twelve pack of beer.

'I think I'm gonna take a shower,' she said and brought the beer back to her mother. 'I put another one in the freezer for you.'

'Thanks.'

'I got paid yesterday. You mind if I take your car and go grocery shopping after I get cleaned up? I could make us dinner.'

'The keys are on the counter. You and me, maybe Evelyn if she gets back in time. We could eat in front of the TV and watch Paul Newman, like a real family.'

'Maybe I'll make lasagna then,' the girl said and walked down the hall and into the bathroom. She locked the door behind her, turned on the light, started water in the sink, and undressed. She stood in front of the mirror and looked at her face. The cut above her eye was swollen, but it was so close to her eyebrow it wasn't that noticeable. Her nose and chin were swollen as well, but there was nothing she could do about that. There was dried blood caked around the cut, and she took a wash cloth from the bathtub and put it under the water. Her face was sore, but the cut didn't look too bad once the blood was off.

She started the shower, grabbed the shampoo, held it in her hand, then turned off the light and in the darkness stepped into the tub, under the warm water, and sat down.

Her leg was sore and the bruise looked worse. Dark blue and purple and yellow. She put the shampoo next to her, felt around for a bar of soap, and washed her body. She let the water flow down. She sat back, opened the shampoo, poured some into her hand, and washed her hair. Then she turned the water hotter, curled in a ball directly under it, and finally let herself cry.

13

SAFEWAY

As she backed her mom's Chevy onto the street she had the soda wedged between her legs. She'd added fresh ice to it and the last of the vodka. The radio was set on AM country classics. Her black hair was still wet and pulled back with hair pins. She was dressed in a pair of jeans and a faded black T-shirt that read 'Johnny Cash Live at San Quentin' in white block letters. She wore her mother's large, mirror-lensed sunglasses and ran the A/C in the car on full.

The neighborhood was mostly Mexican. The majority of the white families who had once lived there had moved to the suburbs, to gated communities and planned estate housing. When she was a kid it had been different. She could walk down the street by herself at night. Her mom would send her and her sister to the 7-11 with money for milk or candy or soda. Now her mom wouldn't even drive there. She would go to a store two miles away. They had installed window locks and bolt locks on the door. They had gotten a dog from the pound, a German Shepherd mix they named The Hulk. The car had been stolen twice, their house broken into once, and their barbecue was chained to the back porch after it had been stolen for the second time.

She parked in the lot in front of Safeway, but left the engine running until she had finished the soda. She cut the engine, opened the door, threw the ice from the cup onto the asphalt, and got out. It was Saturday, crowded, and she had to park in the back. She left her sunglasses on, found a stick of gum in her purse, and went inside.

Under the fluorescent lights, she saw them, the people, the kids, the shoppers yelling and running around all talking and in a hurry. A lady on an intercom announced: 'Fryer breasts on sale for $1.70 a pound. Betty Crocker cake mix on sale for $1.99 a box . . .'

Her anxiety began as soon as she entered, her heart racing, her stomach beginning to knot. The liquor section was across the store, she could see the sign. She took a basket and headed in that direction.

She bought a half a pint of vodka, put the bottle in her purse, and began to walk up and down aisles with her grocery list. Soon she saw a large woman with three kids. One kid was in the cart and the other two were next to the woman. The girl was in the spaghetti section and they were farther down in the soup section walking towards her. Then they stopped next to her and the woman put two boxes of spaghetti into her cart.

As she went down the aisle she watched the woman, her large body waddling, her kids talking and surrounding her. There was a dark stain on the seat of the woman's sweat pants. Her period, the girl thought to herself. She wanted to tell the woman, let her know. Run up to her and whisper in her ear. Watch her kids and let the woman go to the bathroom. But she just stood there and her nerves began again because of it. The fluorescent lights came back. So did the people. The store was full. The lines were long and slow. A Mexican family was walking up the aisle speaking Spanish. The lady with the dull voice began announcing specials over the intercom again. The girl walked down a few aisles before she set the basket down in front of the bathroom. Hiding herself in a stall she opened the bottle and took a drink.

When she got back *The Hustler* had just begun. Her mother was rubbing BenGay on her legs and smoking a cigarette. Dark blue marks from varicose veins ran up and down her thighs and calves.

'I'm glad you went to the store,' she said during a commercial. 'I couldn't do it today. I'm beat. Maybe I'm wrong about dealing, maybe you should get a job off your feet. My legs have gone to hell.'

'I'm already getting them,' the girl said. She was in the kitchen making the lasagna.

'You're too young.'

'Your legs don't look that bad.'

'Ha!' her mom said as she rubbed her legs.

'What's happening now?' the girl said.

'I don't know exactly, just a lot of talking and pool. I haven't been paying attention. I need one more favor from you, and then I'll let you be. You mind making a batch of hot water and Epsom salts for my feet? If you do that, I'll be about perfect. You cooking me dinner, us together watching Paul Newman, and Evelyn coming home soon.'

The girl finished the last layer of the lasagna and put it in the oven. There was a small plastic tub in the garage and she grabbed it, mixed the salts and hot tap water into it, and set it down by her mother's feet. Then she went back to the kitchen, opened a beer, and watched the TV from there.

'You still seeing that guy?'

'You mean Tom?' her mother asked and lit a cigarette.

'The tall guy. Black hair. I only saw him once or twice.'

'That's Tom. He was still married but I didn't find that out until later. What a grease ball. I could go into it but I'd rather look at Paul Newman. How about you and Jimmy?'

'I don't know.'

'I only see you here three times a week now. You gonna move in with him?'

'I don't know what I'm gonna do.'

'Jesus, I'd be lonely if you and Evelyn both moved out.'

'I don't think I will. Anyway, let's just watch Paul Newman,' the girl said, taking a cigarette from her mom's pack on the table. She lit it and sat down.

After supper they watched *Butch Cassidy and the Sundance Kid*. Her mother fell asleep and the girl drank coffee and ate ice cream and watched Paul Newman ride alongside Robert Redford. The two joking back and forth and robbing banks and hiding out together in Bolivia.

When the movie ended she woke her mother and helped her to bed. She put a glass of water on her night stand and made sure her alarm clock was set and the curtains shut.

She went to the bathroom, got nail polish remover, nail polish, and an emery board, then filled her coffee from the pot on the stove and sat back down. She had toilet paper balled up between her toes and was blowing on her nails when she heard the front door open. Her sister Evelyn walked in carrying a sleeping bag and a backpack.

'What are you doing here?' she said excitedly.

'It's a Paul Newman marathon. *Nobody's Fool* is on.'

'No kidding?' her sister said and flopped down on the couch. She was sixteen, with the same black hair and blue eyes and thin body as her sister. 'But he's old in this one.'

'Yeah, but he's still cute.'

'Cute in a gross old man sorta way. They shown *The Sting* yet?'

'No, it's coming up after this one, I think. They just finished *Butch Cassidy and the Sundance Kid.*'

'I like Robert Redford better in that one,' Evelyn said and took off her shoes. 'But I like Paul Newman better in *The Sting*. I'm so stoned right now. We went up to the lake. Me and Junior and a couple of his friends. His brother rented a house boat.'

'That sounds nice.'

'What smells so good? Mom didn't cook, did she?'

'No, I made lasagna.'

'I've hardly eaten all weekend,' she said and went to the kitchen and came back with a Coke, a plate of lasagna, and a package of saltines. 'You still staying with what's his face?'

'Jimmy.'

'If you ask me he's a loser.'

'I'm looking at Paul Newman right now.'

'He's too old in this one.'

'I'd go out with him.'

'That's sick, that's like Mr Renton when he lived next door. Imagine if you were having sex with him. He'd be stuttering, then his teeth would fall out and hit you on the head.'

'That's sick.'

'That's what I'm trying to tell you. You want to see something?'

'I'm not sure.'

'It hurt so bad I started crying.' She pulled her top off. She turned on the lamp next to her. There were silver rings in her nipples. 'I got them pierced. It hurt so bad. Worse than my tattoo. It's lucky I don't have to wear a bra 'cause that would kill.'

'My God, that looks painful.'

'We were drunk and Junior talked me into it. He has this friend and he did it at his shop for free. I might take them out. It's supposed to feel good but I don't know. They say it's not supposed to hurt for too long. I've been putting hydrogen peroxide on it three or four times a day, but still.'

'Do you have to sleep on your back?'

'Yeah, but I like sleeping on my back.'

'The show's on again.' Paul Newman was in an old pickup truck. His kid and grandkid were there, sitting next to him. There was snow on the ground and they were having a hard time starting the beat-up truck.

'How's the Plaza?'

'All right, but I should try to get in somewhere where the tips are better. Plus that place has the worst food in the world. At least a couple times a day I get yelled at 'cause of it. Even the drunk people complain.'

'You should waitress in a fancy place and then you'd make a fortune.'

'I should.'

'Junior and I are going to move down to Mexico. His grandfather just died and he's gonna get something like five thousand dollars. Can you imagine having that kind of money? You can rent a place on the beach down there for cheap. We could probably live a couple years on that alone. Plus Junior's been making these necklaces and wristbands. Here's what the wristbands look like.' She put her wrist underneath the lamp and showed them to her. 'He's been selling them at school. On the way down we might go to LA and sell them along the beach for extra cash.'

'I'd tell you to stay in school, but I hated that place.' The girl took a cigarette from her mom's pack on the coffee table and lit it. 'But I should have graduated or at least gotten my GED.'

'Maybe we could do it together.'

'If you want to, I really will. Jesus, you know if Paul Newman lived next door, even the way he is in, say, the *Color of Money* or *The Verdict*, maybe even as old as he is in this one, I'd still marry him.'

'Maybe he'd have his social security check like Junior's grandma, and he'd spend it on you. Take you to Dennys or Carrows.' Evelyn laughed again.

'I'm serious,' the girl said. 'We would drive down to Mexico in his pickup. We'd stop at all the tourist places along the way. Then we'd rent a little house overlooking a beach and we'd listen to music and play cards and go swimming. At night we'd go eat at a restaurant and walk around town and sit outside at a bar and you and Junior would be there.'

'I bet Junior and him would get along great.'

'And we'd all drink Margaritas.'

'Maybe Junior could get a job working for him.'

'Maybe we could get a house next to each other.'

'Matching houses,' her sister said giggling. 'Matching houses and matching cars. Everything exactly the same. We'd even dress the same. Now that would be something.'

THE BARBECUE

When *The Sting* finished she drove her sister to Junior's mother's apartment. When she returned she went into the bedroom they shared and put a tape of Patti Page's greatest hits into the cassette player. It played softly and she sat at an old card table she had by the window. She turned on a lamp and found a pen and a blank piece of notebook paper.

Saturday
Last night was worse than two weeks ago and worse than the time in the motel. It'll never change I know that. You are stupid. You are a stupid and horrible disgusting person. If you worked harder maybe you would amount to something. If you weren't so weak and so stupid you wouldn't be with such a horrible person. You don't even have your GED. Everyone graduates from high school. You'd have to be a moron not to. So you are a moron. All the girls at work have graduated from high school. And look at them. You're worse than them. And now what are you going to do? You're in a bad fix and you know it. You're too scared to do anything about it. You're too scared to even tell anyone. Don't put it off like you put everything else off, this time you can't! You're a bad person. You've ruined everything good that's ever happened to you and helped everything bad. You're going to hell. No matter what happens you're going to live forever in hell.

When she finished, she stopped the music and took the piece of paper and walked outside. Their dog, The Hulk, was underneath the picnic table, sleeping.

'Hello, little boy,' she said and looked at him. 'Are you all right out here on your own? You want to sleep inside with me?'

The dog got up and walked out to her and sat by her feet.

'I guess that's a yes,' she said and petted him again.

She took a match from a box on the table, and lit the paper. When it took hold, she opened the old barbecue and threw the paper inside. They hadn't cooked anything on it in years. One of her mother's boyfriends had parted it out. The grill was missing and so were the burners. There was nothing in it except a deep pile of ash from at least a hundred notes she'd let burn there.

FLYING J

The next day as she watched TV a car pulled into the drive. It was early evening. She was laying on the couch in her underwear when she heard it. She hoped it was her mother, but knew in her heart it wasn't. She walked into the kitchen and looked out the window and saw Jimmy Bodie's parked car and him walking up the lawn.

He knocked on the door. She stood silent in the kitchen, and prayed he would give up and leave, but he wouldn't. She didn't know what to do. Her nerves began to go. He knocked again and then again, and finally he walked around the house and looked in each window. She tried to move, to hide, but she was too scared to do anything and finally he saw her in the kitchen.

'Come on,' he begged her. 'Answer the door.'

The girl didn't say anything. She just stood motionless. He kept staring at her and he kept calling for her. He began knocking on the window. She began to hyperventilate. She tried to breathe. She tried to calm down. She forced herself to look at him. There were tears running down his face. He looked like he was dying. And this went on. Him staring at her, and her staring at him and then finally she gave in, walked to the entry hall, and unlocked the door.

'You know I'm sorry,' he said in a cracked voice. 'Don't you? Don't you know that?' He was pale and stood there shaky and hollow. His hair was combed badly. There were globs of pomade in it.

23

She noticed the dried toothpaste on his lips and chin.

'It all seems like a fucking nightmare,' he said and paused. He looked at her. His voice fell to an almost whisper. 'I just woke up. I'm so sorry. I'll quit taking speed. I swear I will. I swear.'

The girl looked at him but remained silent. She tried to calm her breathing.

'What are you doing now?' he asked her.

'Watching TV,' she said weakly.

'Can I come in?'

'I don't know.'

'Then maybe I could take you out,' he said.

'I gotta work tomorrow,' she told him.

'I won't keep you out late,' he said. He opened the screen door and walked in. He put his arm around her.

'Don't,' she said as strong as she could.

'Look,' he told her. 'Let me take you out to eat at least. And there's a party in the desert if you want to go to that.'

'I can't.'

'Please,' he said gently.

He took her hand and led her inside. He shut the door behind them and fell to his knees in front of her. He began kissing her feet.

'What are you doing?' she said nearly crying. He would never leave, she knew that then. If she did stay home, he'd stay too, and then they would end up in her bedroom.

'I'm starting at the bottom where I belong,' he said.

'I know I can't drink, but I didn't hit you and handcuff you to a bed.'

Jimmy stood up and tried to hold her. 'Look, I feel horrible about it. You know I do. I'm through with that shit. I told you. I swear.'

'Do you really promise?'

'If you quit drinking so much.'

'I'm trying,' she said. 'I really am trying.'

'Then will you go out with me?' he asked her.

She moved away from him. She could hardly breathe.

In the car she sat near the window, as far from him as she could, and let her arm hang out as he drove them onto the highway. She could see the casino lights in the distance begin to fade.

It was almost night when they came upon a stalled pick-up truck in the middle of a two lane highway. There was an old man inside the cab trying to start it.

Jimmy pulled the car over and got out and spoke to the man. Together they pushed the truck to the side of the road. He opened the hood and within minutes had the truck running. The old man shook his hand and drove away.

'What was wrong?' the girl asked when he got back in.

'A wire fell off the solenoid. He was an old timer. He didn't have a goddamn tooth in him.'

'Not any?'

'No, but he seemed all right. He was nice enough. He invited us to his house.'

'He did?'

'Yeah.'

'Are we going?'

'Hell, I'd rather dig a grave,' he said and laughed.

*

They stopped at a Flying J truck stop, went into the restaurant, and sat at a booth that looked out upon an endless parking lot of tractor-trailers. A waitress came by and Jimmy ordered a beer and a shot of Jim Beam. There were dozens of truck drivers around them and a band playing in the lounge next to them.

'Whose party is this?' she asked.

'It's some sort of skinhead rally. They got generators out there and bands and supposedly kegs. But if it's anything like I've seen, none of it will probably work. I'm starting to think every single one of them is an idiot. A couple days ago I went with Warren to a house where these skinheads live. They're all sitting around drinking beer listening to music. They had the TV on, and I hate TV, you know that. They had guns laid out on the table. The table cloth was a fucking Nazi flag. We got to drinking beers and talking and really all they wanted to do was beat the shit out of some beaners. Not any particular ones, just drive around and pound on some poor fucker.'

The waitress came. She put the drinks down, he paid her and drank the shot in one swallow.

'That's pathetic, you know? What's the point of that? They're fucking morons. Most of these guys are low lifes, criminals, and you're supposed to trust them? Trust them with your life? They're disorganized and untrustworthy. I don't think I'd hang out with any of them if it weren't for the fact that we're on the same side.

'Even Matt Hale, the old leader of the World Church of the Creator. I used to read about him. I used to read things he'd put out. He graduated from college, he went to law school. He seemed smarter than the rest. And shit, I just read he got busted for trying to hire some undercover agent to kill a judge. He was in court 'cause somebody else owned the World Church of the Creator name. They can't even get that figured out. They can't even do that right, and then instead of just changing the name he tries to kill the judge. All over the rights of a name.'

Sweat was forming on his brow, and he was beginning to have a hard time sitting still. 'And Hitler? I mean, he killed how many of his own people by starting a war? He should of just sealed up Germany and led by example. Exported the Jews if he hated them, but don't kill them. It'll always fail if you do that. People will always come back after you. And then if you believe all the white supremacists, they say the Holocaust didn't happen, that it's all Jew lies. They say there's no way it was six million that were killed. But I don't think Jews could really convince everyone in the world that there were six million when there wasn't. I mean, could they? They don't have that much power, do they? Someone would find out, some historian would discover that there wasn't that many. He'd find out just 'cause he was a historian or a journalist, and that's his job, to search for truth. And why pick on Jews? Really, why? I don't get it. They never ruin neighborhoods or start gangs, do they? And Hitler, he was a crazed lunatic. How could you have him as your leader? You know he sent little kids to fight, did experiments on Jewish prisoners. Horrible things. Shooting them full of crazy drugs, doing fucked-up awful surgeries. Sex changes, amputations, they'd take organs out. For no reason they'd do it. Just to experiment. They'd rape and kill women. I can't see how a guy could condone rape. How can that guy be called a hero? I don't want the niggers and the Mexicans 'cause they don't do shit but ruin neighborhoods, but I say export the motherfuckers. Don't do it by beating up some old beaner or putting a cross on a black guy's lawn. Wearing white hoods, I mean,

Christ. They're the laziest bunch of morons I've ever seen. And to think I had a fucking swastika put on you. I'm sorry for that. I really am. I'll pay to have that removed. I'm so goddamn stupid sometimes.'

He stopped talking when he saw the waitress coming towards them with the food. He drank the rest of his beer as she set the plates on the table. He ordered another shot and beer and pushed the food to the center of the table. His hands were unable to stay still. His fingers shook horribly as he tried to get a cigarette from the pack. The girl looked at her food and slowly began eating.

'I mean, look at Vegas. The population's almost tripled in twenty years. That means from when you were born it went from around 400,000 people in the whole county to maybe 1,700,000 now. It was a dump to begin with, then you add all the fucking new people. And the Mexicans come in like fog, cover everything, get in everywhere. They fuck up their country and then they come here. Our border controls are fucked. The INS is fucked. They should stay and fix their own fucking country. You have to do something, don't you? Pretty soon they're gonna ruin everything. Leaving dirty diapers in parking lots, pouring motor oil down drains, throwing trash in the reservoirs, ruining houses, neighbor-hoods. The fucking rich people start it all and then they go and live in the goddamn suburbs in gated communities. They never have any contact with them in the first place except when they need their lawns mowed or their houses cleaned or food served. Put all the Mexicans back in Mexico. And the blacks? They have no respect for themselves. Their men abandon their women. Look at my old neighborhood. The Mexicans and the blacks moved in and now it's a fucking cesspool. My grandma got so scared when her neighborhood went to shit that now she lives in an old folks' home. My grandpa built her goddamn house by himself in the 1950s. The whole thing for her, just the way she wanted it. Brick by fucking brick, after work he did it. He was a damn welder. All day long he was busting his ass for someone else and then he comes home and builds her a house. She hated leaving, she loved that house, but there were three murders on her street in less than five years. She had to get an alarm system. My dad put bars on her windows. In the end everyone was too scared about her being there and finally we made her leave. You don't see that happening in white neighborhoods, do you?

'My dad used to take me outside on the lawn and grab me by the neck and push my face an inch away from dog shit if I ever mouthed off. He must have done that till I was nineteen. He'd take me out there in my underwear, before school, it didn't matter. I hate that fucking cocksucker, but still, I have a job, I pay taxes, I have a retirement plan, I'm saving for a house. My car's insured and I vote. I have a clean record. I give money to my mom. I have money in the bank. I mow my aunt's lawn and visit my grandma. So how can you say that the blacks are forever ruined 'cause they've had a rough go?'

The waitress came back with his beer and whiskey and set it on the table. He drank the shot and watched her walk away.

'She looks like Faith Hill,' the girl said and forced herself to smile.

'Who's that?' Jimmy said and lit another cigarette with his trembling hands.

'The country singer,' she said and ate the chicken fried steak with mashed potatoes and carrots. She looked out the window at a trucker and a woman walking towards the parking lot. The man had a gut and wore a cowboy hat. He had his arm around the woman.

'You ever think about being a truck driver?'

'I'd hate sitting on my ass all day. It makes you lazy as hell. Faith Hill, which song does she sing?'

'"Breathe" or something like that. It doesn't sound country to me.'

'I can't eat,' he said. He put his cigarette out and took a long drink of beer.

'You need to rest.'

'Maybe,' he said. 'You know we should move. Head up north, for real this time. Get a place in Montana, somewhere like that. Away from all this.' He put his hand up in the air, waving until he caught the waitress's attention. She came back over and he ordered another shot from her.

'Maybe she's Faith Hill's sister,' the girl said.

'Maybe,' Jimmy said and lit another cigarette. 'I wonder if that band in the lounge is any good?'

'We could stay here.'

'Sorry about going off like that.'

'You're just talking, it's better than keeping it in,' she said and put her fork down. 'This is really good. Sometimes truck stops have the best food.'

'I like this song. It's an old Merle Haggard song,' Jimmy said. His eyes began to water. 'Music's saved my ass so many times.'

'You got more records than anyone I've ever seen. If you don't mind staying, could I get a piece of pie?'

'I don't care,' he said and looked at a waitress across the way. They sat silent for a time, then he got out of the booth and stood up. He took out two twenty-dollar bills and set them on the table. 'I'll be back. You get whatever you want.'

When the waitress came she got a to-go box for his dinner and ordered a piece of peach pie and a refill on her coffee. She stared out into the parking lot and tried to think about what to do. She thought about getting a room before he got back. A room under a different name. Spending the night there, hiding, then calling her sister or mom in the morning. Or maybe she could catch a ride with a trucker. Maybe the bus stopped there. She wasn't sure what to do and it made her nervous. When the waitress came back with the pie she couldn't eat it.

She waited a half hour for him, then paid the bill and left the restaurant. She walked into the lounge and looked for him there. She went to the gift shop and to the TV lounge and then walked outside to the lot where the car had been parked. She saw him then, in the distance near a lamp post. He was sitting on the asphalt leaning against a concrete barrier.

The moon was beginning to show and she could see it rising. There was a cool breeze starting. When she got to him she stood above him and stared in silence as he smoked a cigarette. She could see he had been crying. There were five or six cigarette butts next to him and an open can of beer.

'I thought you'd left,' she said and sat down across from him.

'Sorry,' he said.

'What's wrong?'

'I don't know,' he said. 'I got so many goddamn thoughts.'

'You're tired,' she said and looked at him. 'You need to go to bed.'

'I don't know,' he said. He took a drink off the beer. 'I'd like to murder the motherfucker.'

'Who?'

'My old man.'

'You need to sleep.'

'I just slept for thirty-six hours.'

'I don't know then.'

'I remember this time when my mom was out of town visiting her sister. This was when I was ten, maybe twelve. My little sister was taking a bath. She was probably six or seven. My dad had this thing about water around the bathroom. Water on the floor. Anyway she gets out of the tub and runs around the house, then gets back in the tub, gets out, and runs around the house, you know?' He paused and wiped the tears from his eyes. 'Just little kid stuff. He was in the family room watching TV. I was in there, too. For a long time he didn't notice her, didn't pay attention to her. I did. I saw it, but I didn't do anything. I don't know why. Did I want her to get in trouble? I don't know. I mean, I was young, too. I don't know what the fuck I was thinking. Finally he sees her naked and wet running around the room. He yells at her and she screams and runs back into the tub. Five or ten minutes later she comes running back out doing the same thing, and I remember sitting there thinking, "Jesus Christ, Jessica, what the hell are you doing? Get back in the fucking tub." I remember watching her, scared for her. And then allthe sudden, he sees her again and he gets up and starts yelling at her. He follows her into the bathroom. He sees all the water on the carpet, and sees all the water on the bathroom floor. I can still remember him yelling at her. I got up and walked down the hall. I heard him pick her up and her scream. I looked inside and he was holding her by her ankles. He was yelling at her and she was screaming. He started dunking her head in the tub water. Over and over. I was screaming at him, he looked at me and yelled at me. Then he let go of her ankles, and when he did I ran for the door. But I didn't make it.'

'I'm sorry,' she said.

He began crying again. 'And that was nothing. That was nothing. That was just one night. There were others.'

'Come on,' she said and stood up. 'Let's get out of here. Let's go home.'

He wiped his eyes and finished his beer.

'All right,' he said.

She held out her hand to help him stand, and he reached for it.

They walked to the car and set off for home. Once they had got out of the Flying J and onto the highway, though, he had opened a beer and taken a drink off the half pint he'd bought her, and changed his mind. All of a sudden he wanted to go to the party in the desert. He turned the car around, drove back to the truck stop, and bought a twelve pack of beer and a fifth of Jim Beam. He put in a mixed tape of Johnny Cash and had the girl drive.

'The crazy thing', he said, 'is that Johnny Cash wrote that song "San Quentin" for the guys in there, the inmates, and just for that one show. During the concert he talks about the song, then plays it for them. The prisoners like it so much he asks if they want to hear it again, and of course they yell their asses off, 'cause he'd just written a song about them, so of course they want to hear it again. So he does it again and everyone goes ape shit. The craziest thing is, when you buy the record, it's on there, both times. Back to back.'

She rolled down her window and rested her arm on the top of the door while she drove. The breeze rushing past her, the night air on her arm, blowing through her hair.

'You remember when we saw him at that outdoor place in San Diego?'

'Yeah,' she said.

'We stayed at that motel. That was one of the best times in my life. I remember it that way. You and me sleeping the whole day away. And then us getting dressed up and going out to eat and then seeing that show.'

'He was good, too,' the girl said.

'He was fucking great. Even for being such an old timer, he was good.'

Jimmy took a flashlight from the glove box and turned it on. He was looking at a flyer. 'I hope all these guys aren't a bunch of gun shooting idiots. Do you remember that skinhead party where there was a band in the backyard and the sliding glass door got broken by those two drunk girls fighting?'

'I remember that,' she said.

'I don't know if I told you, but I had this conversation with a guy there. He says that the cops are on his ass 'cause they think he threw a Molotov cocktail at some black lady's car. But he tells me, "No way did I do it, man." He doesn't know me from anyone. I'd never met the man before in my life. I could have been an undercover cop. He was drunk, a real moron, you know? So I ask him, "Why do they think you did it?" And he looks at me and says, "They're picking on me 'cause I'm a skinhead. If it was me that did it, if I'd of thrown it, it would have torched the fucking car. There'd be nothing left. Those dumbfuck cops say it hit the trunk and could've gotten to the gas tank and so I could be up for attempted murder. But the fucker landed on the hood. The cops don't know shit. Maybe I was there, but I didn't make it. If I made it, it would've exploded. The guys I know can't hit anything, but I got the arm." He was that fucking dumb. I mean, he couldn't even keep his story straight. And he couldn't keep his mouth shut, not for even one night, not even in front of someone who doesn't give a shit about him or what he does, in front of someone who doesn't even know him.'

35

'You mind if I have a beer?' the girl said. Her nerves were beginning to go. They were driving so far away from town. She had to work in the morning. She knew he wouldn't want to leave the party. She'd miss work, she'd be put back on probation, maybe this time she'd be fired.

He handed her a beer. She opened it, took a drink from it, and put it between her legs.

'You're not gonna pass out on me, are you?'

'No,' she said. 'It's just one beer.'

'You're sure?' he said.

'I won't.'

'If you do, do it in the car so I don't have to look everywhere for you.'

'I won't.'

He finished the half pint, threw it out the window, opened the fifth of whiskey, and took a drink off it. 'You know, Johnny Cash never spent any real time in jail. He wrote all that shit about it and about Vietnam by reading books. He wrote books himself. Now that's something.' He turned on the flashlight again, glanced at the flyer, then looked at the mile markers passing them and told the girl the turnoff was just after the next marker. She slowed when she came upon it. She saw the road leading from the highway, and turned onto the dirt and gravel surface.

They were in the desert now with nothing around them. No buildings or stores or gas stations for miles. They drove for twenty minutes on the dirt road. The girl drank the beer and got another one. She almost started crying.

She wasn't listening to him anymore. She just pictured them driving on a mountain road, in the middle of nowhere. She'd open the door, and without him even noticing, jump out. It didn't matter to her if she fell off the cliff or rolled down a mountain or got hit by an oncoming car. Just the thought of jumping calmed her. The thought and the image of his tail lights slowly flickering and fading away and her body falling, crashing, and disappearing.

'There sure ain't nothing out there,' he told her as he looked out the window. 'I wonder if any crazy old hermit ever lived out here? Or some old miner or hippie?'

'Do you see the fires in the distance up there?'

'Yeah,' he said.

'They look strange, don't they?'

'I guess.'

'How many you think there are?'

'Maybe seven,' he said.

'I got to work tomorrow,' she said.

'I know,' he said. 'I don't plan on being here all night.'

'Okay,' she said.

'Just park before the first car. That way we can get out easy.'

As the fires came into focus they could see lines of cars in front of them, and she parked behind the first car she came to. He got out and put the whiskey in his coat pocket. She put two beers in her purse and he carried the rest.

There were dozens of cars lined up along the road, and they walked past them for almost a hundred yards before they came to the party. There was a band playing on a makeshift pallet stage. There was a fire going on each side of it. There were people around them, talking. They walked to where they could see the band playing.

The singer had his shirt off, and had tattoos covering his chest, arms, and neck. The music was fast and he was screaming as hard as he could while the rest of the band played. When the song ended, the thirty or so people watching cheered and screamed. People threw beer into the air and onto each other. There were kegs that sat near the stage and the people there were drunk, laughing and yelling. There were tents and separate fires in the distance that she could just make out.

A kid walked past them with blood coming down the side of his head. In one hand he was carrying a beer and in the other a bloody shirt. He was laughing, talking to a couple other kids as he passed.

'Jesus,' the girl said and moved closer to Jimmy. 'Did you see that?'

'What a fucking idiot.'

'He should go to a doctor.'

'He probably doesn't feel a thing,' Jimmy said and turned to her. 'Stay here for a couple minutes. I'll go look around and see if Warren's here.'

'Can I come with you?' she asked. 'I don't want to just stand here by myself.'

'I'll be back in a couple minutes. I'm gonna search the fires. You look around here where the band's playing. Don't worry, if you find them, tell them to stay here with you until I get back.'

He then turned and walked into the darkness. The band played another song. The girl opened her purse and took a beer from it. She lit a cigarette and began looking for their friends.

A trail of men passed her dressed in matching German military uniforms. One kid wore desert goggles and had a short black mustache. One had his hair completely shaved, and the other wore an

39

old German army helmet. They were drunk and talking loudly. The band finished another song and the crowd cheered again.

She finished her beer and took the last can she had and opened it. She was beginning to feel drunk and her nerves eased. The band started another song and she saw her friend Nan Endrick in the distance walking towards her.

'It's hard to believe we're out in the middle of nowhere,' the girl said.

'It was raining last year,' Nan said. She was under five feet tall and must have gained fifty pounds in the last year. Her arms were tattooed, her hair was one step away from shaved and dyed black and blonde. She wore Levi cutoffs and a men's undershirt.

'It's been going for three days straight. Are you staying the night?'

'I have to go to work in the morning. Did Jimmy find you?'

'He pointed to where you were. I didn't think you'd make it.'

'We weren't sure we could.'

'I'll show you where we're camped,' she said and they walked down a trail to an old army-issue tent, where the three men – Warren Cooper, Jimmy, and Keith Henry – sat inside at a portable picnic table drinking beer, talking. The smell of speed mixed with the smell of beef stew cooking on a Coleman stove and filled the tent.

'We're all gonna take a walk to the canyon,' Warren said when he saw the girls. He took a backpack that lay on the tent floor and filled it with bottles of beer. He put two flashlights in a side pocket. He turned off the camping stove, covered the stew, and shut off the lantern.

With the moon out and almost full, they didn't use the flashlights, and Nan and the girl drifted behind while the three men disappeared in front of them.

'He's good looking,' Nan said quietly.

'Who?'

'Keith.'

'I don't know—'

'You never know anything when it comes to men,' Nan said.

'Maybe,' the girl said.

The three men stopped and stood looking out over the canyon. There was a dry creek bed at the bottom and rough rock on the sides of it. The moon and the stars shone down on the sage brush with a pale blue light.

'It's the sort of place Sitting Bull might have relaxed at if he ever had to come down this far,' Jimmy said and opened a beer. 'He'd of probably sat back and smoked a pipe and thought things over. Tried to figure out what to do.'

'He probably would have fucked some dirty squaw and then thrown her off the edge,' Keith said.

'Jesus,' Warren said. 'That's an image.'

The two men laughed.

'You're an idiot,' Jimmy said calmly. 'Sitting Bull was a hero. He fought like a motherfucker. He didn't want anything from us. Maybe guns, maybe he wanted them, but that was only 'cause he had to get them to beat us. If it weren't for disease and guns, who knows what would have happened? He didn't want to live on a reservation, live on shitty land with nothing to do but start drinking and wait for handouts. I got no problem with the Indians back then. It's now that they're all fucked up, and the government's to blame as much as anything. But they have to quit drinking. That's something. If they did that, they'd probably have most of it licked. Sitting Bull, he was nothing like you think. He's one of the great ones. His people believed in him. He didn't want to integrate. He didn't want his people to go to our church and be shit on or go to our schools and get laughed at. We should have cut off a state or two and let them be.'

'I don't give a shit about Indians,' Keith said. 'I don't give a fuck what anybody says.'

Jimmy took a long drink from his beer and sat down.

'I don't mind Indians,' Warren said.

'You wouldn't,' Keith said and laughed.

They all looked out at the night, at the moon and the stars.

Jimmy leaned over to Warren.

'You know the Indians,' he said quietly, 'they used to chase deer or buffalo or rabbits and herd them towards a cliff, and the animals would be so freaked out that they'd jump right off. They'd have other people from the tribe – the women and kids probably – below, and their job was to make sure that once the deer or rabbits or whatever landed that they were all dead. They'd have clubs with them. Then they'd clean them, tan the hides, and have a huge celebration that'd last for days.'

'Jesus,' Warren said, looking out over the canyon. 'Can you imagine seeing that from below? All them buffalo diving off cliffs. Did they have horses? How'd they herd them off?'

'I'm not sure how they did it, but they didn't have horses for a long time, so I'd imagine in the beginning they did it without them somehow.'

'The stupid fuckers didn't have horses or much of anything before the white man,' Keith said.

Jimmy threw his empty beer bottle as hard as he could down into the canyon and took a new one from Warren's pack.

'I don't like wasting my time talking about Indians,' Keith said.

'Then don't talk,' Jimmy said. He was no longer able to sit still. His hands were twitching. 'You shouldn't be allowed to say a god-damn thing anyway.'

She passed out sometime in the night and when she woke she turned her head towards a light, a lantern, and in a haze she saw Jimmy talking to a woman she didn't recognize. He was saying things to her, but she couldn't understand what, and then he began kissing the woman and his hand went up her leg. The girl closed her eyes and when she opened them again she was alone in the darkness of the tent.

She sat up, got herself together the best she could, found her purse and coat, and left. She went by the tents and passed the fires where people were still drinking and talking, and then by the empty stage, and finally passed the long row of parked cars, including Jimmy's, and began walking faster. She'd have to hitchhike. She didn't know if anyone drove that road at night, but she hoped she'd catch a ride before daylight. At least before the party broke and everyone left.

She stood alongside the two lane road for an hour, but only a single truck passed and it didn't stop. Two cars had come down the gravel road from the party, leaving. When she saw the headlights from them, she laid down in the dirt behind sage brush and waited until they were gone.

Just after four o'clock in the morning, a tractor-trailer passed and saw her, then slowed and pulled over. She ran towards the cab as fast as she could and without hesitation got in, sat in the passenger seat, and shut the door.

'I ain't supposed to have riders,' the old man who was the driver said. 'I could get fired for it, but I ain't about to let a girl sit out in the middle of the desert alone. My wife would have my hide if I did that.' He was smoking a cigarette as he spoke, his face lit only by the dim dashboard lights. She guessed he was in his sixties. He was a big man who was overweight. The radio was playing and he was dressed in a white, short-sleeved western shirt and black jeans. He was balding and wore glasses with half-inch-thick lenses and steel rims.

'You all right?'

'Thanks for picking me up.'

'My name is T.J. Watson. You can call me Tom if you want. What's your name?' He looked in the side mirror, put the truck into first, and started them back on the road.

'Allison Johnson.'

'If you don't mind me asking, Allison, what in the hell are you doing all the way out here?'

'I was at a party. There was a huge party in the desert.'

'Didn't feel like staying, huh?"

'Not really,' she said. She looked about the cab. It was warm. The seat was comfortable and there was the smell of cigarettes and coffee. He was listening to talk radio.

'My boy used to go to parties in the mountains. We live outside Reno, me and my wife. He and I rebuilt a 1972 Ford pick up together. We used it for hunting and camping mostly. He used to take that thing up into the mountains and him and his friends would have parties. I suppose a lot like the party you were at. He'd bring up his chainsaw and cut up some old fallen trees and start a big fire. Probably drank beer and did who knows what. You want a splash of coffee?'

'Okay,' the girl said.

'The thermos is next to you and there should be a clean cup behind your seat.'

She reached around the seat and found the cup, then opened the thermos and poured the coffee into it.

'Do you need a refill?' she asked timidly.

'No,' he said. 'I'm almost through, and I'm so jittery I'm like a goddamn jack rabbit. Listen, I'm done at the Flying J. They give us a room there. I hope that will be far enough. You heading back to town?'

'Yeah,' she said.

'There's probably a bus or something. Probably catch a ride easy then. Or at least wait until it's light so you can see what you're getting into. It can be dangerous, hitchhiking. I wouldn't recommend it to anyone. Especially a young girl,' he said and fell silent.

'Does your wife ever ride with you?' she asked after awhile.

'She used to all the time,' he answered. 'When she retired I got on as a long haul driver for a different company, and they didn't mind me having a rider. She must have gone with me for five or six years. All over the country. We've seen most of the highlights. Then she got tired of it, so I got a job with a company out of Reno. That was maybe five years ago. I'm only away two, maybe three nights a week. But I'm retiring in a year anyway.'

'Did she like driving around? I mean at first?'

'I think so. We used to do crossword puzzles. She'd have a couple dictionaries on her lap and we'd do them from every local paper we found. We started listening to books on tape. She'd read novels to me. Westerns mostly. Zane Grey, Louis Lamour. I like a lot of things, but a good western is nice to drive to. That or mysteries. Mysteries pass the time pretty good.'

'I think I'd like that. To see things from here.'

'It ain't a bad life. Better than being in an office or a warehouse or at a desk. It's got its good points and bad points like anything else. I hate to pry, but my wife, she'll be curious about you when I tell her I picked you up. She'll want to know. You get in a fight with your boyfriend? Is that what got you stranded out here?'

'Kind of,' she said and took a drink of her coffee, and then suddenly was crying.

'I'm sorry,' she said in a broken voice.

'There's nothing wrong with crying. You're young, you'll be all right. I know that sounds like a bag of hot air to you right now, but it's true.'

'It doesn't seem to help,' she said.

The man laughed. 'My wife would probably have something better to say.'

'I hate when I cry in front of other people.'

She set the coffee mug between her legs and wiped her eyes.

'There's nothing wrong with crying,' he said and paused. 'My boy, the one I was telling you about – he and his girlfriend were driving home from camping out near Elko. It was maybe three in the afternoon and a driver crossed the median and ran into them. It killed everyone involved. On a Tuesday this happened. In early June. Not a cloud in the sky, the roads were fine. The lady that hit them was alone in the car, and she had three kids at home. She was married and was a teacher for a high school. They say she just fell asleep. It wasn't drinking, and she wasn't on drugs. But her just falling asleep cost me my boy, cost her kids a mom, cost his girlfriend's folks a daughter. Imagine that. All 'cause someone fell asleep. My poor wife could barely get out of bed after it happened. She didn't want to go out on the road either, she just wanted to stay home. So I quit my long haul job and got this one. But I can't even tell you how many nights I've sat in this cab and cried my eyes out. Out of the blue it'll just hit me. Like a breeze or a cough. Just pops up and hits down on you like a hammer, and then you just start crying. Sometimes it gets to where I have to pull the truck over 'cause I can't stop. I just have to close my eyes and lay down in the seats. Or if I'm on this route and I'm in the desert, sometimes I'll just pull over and get out. I'll put on my hiking boots and just start walking. I'm never gone that long, but I feel better when I get back.'

'I'm sorry about your son.'

'Thank you for saying so,' he said. He tuned the station on the radio and turned it up.

'I'm pregnant,' the girl said finally.

'No kidding?' he said and coughed.

'I am.'

'How far are you along?'

'Almost three months.'

'The boy, your boyfriend, what's he say?'

'He doesn't know.'

'You think maybe you should tell him?'

'He's not a good person.'

The girl began crying again.

'You got any family?'

'My mom and my sister.'

'They know?'

'I haven't told anyone.'

'You'd be surprised by people sometimes. People understand a lot more than you give them credit for.'

'Maybe,' she said and looked out the window. 'Does your wife like Reno?'

'She thinks the area is the greatest place on earth. She grew up on a ranch in Washoe Valley. Her folks were cattle people, but then her dad got on at a machine shop and they sold their place and moved into town. I don't think she's ever left except for spending a summer with her aunt in Chicago and traveling around with me when I was on long haul. I'm from Tacoma, Washington. Some of my family still live up there, but I got a job in Reno after I got out of the army. Then I met my wife and we got married and lived in the city for a few years. Then we bought a house ten miles away in the town of Verdi. On the foothills of the Sierras. I'm not a hundred yards from the Truckee River. We got a little place with a yard full of pinyon pines.'

'Sounds beautiful.'

'You should visit sometime. My wife would enjoy the company. She enjoys young people. You ever listen to Art Bell on the radio?'

'The guy that talks about aliens and space ships?'

'That's him.'

'My sister listens to him at night sometimes. In the mornings she'll tell me about what he says. She loves all that sorta thing. *Star Wars* and *The X-Files*, *Lord of the Rings*, all the *Star Treks*.'

'I don't know any of those shows.'

'You'd like *The X-Files*. It's a TV show. If you like Art Bell then you'd really like it. It's full of extra terrestrial stuff. Weird things happen. It's about these two FBI agents who track down aliens. One of the agents believes in it all and everyone thinks he's crazy.

49

So the bosses at the FBI assign him a partner who's a scientist. She's skeptical all the time and really smart and really beautiful and they're always almost falling in love with each other. My sister reads books about that sorta thing. There's that one about getting abducted she just read. It starts with a C, I think.'

'You mean *Communion*?'

'Yeah,' Allison said. 'I think that's the one.'

'My wife read that to me.'

'That stuff freaks me out, but my sister Evelyn, she loves it.'

'The reason I asked is Art Bell's show is going to start in a couple minutes, and I promised the wife I'd listen to it. She has a hard time sleeping at night, so she listens to him, and she likes it when I do too. She takes little notes on it, keeps a pad by the bed and turns on the light when he says something good and pencils it down. Then when I call we can talk about it.'

'Have you ever seen a UFO?'

'No,' he said and laughed.

'I haven't either,' she said. Some time passed and then the girl started crying again, quietly.

'It'll be all right,' the old man said. 'Once you face it, it'll be all right. You got a baby to think about now. Once you admit that, you'll know what to do.'

T. J. Watson gave her twenty dollars and his home address before he said good-bye. They were standing in the parking lot of the Flying J. She hugged the old man and thanked him for the ride. She made him a list of television shows she thought he might like on a blank log page he gave her to write on. He took the note, put it in his wallet, and thanked her. Then slowly he walked towards the motel. He walked with a slight limp and with the soreness of a tired old man. She watched until he went through the doors of the motel and disappeared.

SUNDAY

She went to the fuel counter and asked if they had a bus or a shuttle that ran into Las Vegas. The woman at the counter turned and asked the shift manager, who told her they didn't. She bought a *People* magazine and a small notebook from the trucker's store and went into the restaurant. She sat at the counter and ordered a waffle with bacon and coffee. It was near dawn and she was meant to be at work in an hour, but in her heart she knew then that she'd never go back there.

The waitress came with the food and set it on the table.

'Do you know how I could get back to Vegas?'

The waitress was a short, pale, fifty-year-old woman with gray hair.

'You stuck out here?'

'I am,' Allison said.

'I wouldn't recommend riding with any of them truckers. I have to see them all day. I think I'd rather walk. We're about to do a shift change. I know a couple of the boys in the kitchen who live near the city. I'll see what they say – other than that I don't know.'

The woman left and the girl began eating.

'Justin, one of our cooks, lives in the city,' the waitress said when she returned. 'He told me he's off in twenty minutes and would give you a ride, and he's good enough for that. I'd let him give me a ride home, I guess,' she said, and filled the girl's coffee. 'How did you get stuck all the way out here?'

'My boyfriend,' she said.

'Always is,' the woman said and walked away.

The girl finished her meal, then took the new pad of paper from her purse, and began writing.

Monday

I swear I swear I swear I'll quit drinking. I have to call Mary at work. Why have I waited so long? Should I get an abortion? Maybe the reason I keep waiting is hoping that Jimmy will be different. Or that maybe he'll disappear. Maybe he'll just die. Maybe he died last night. Am I horrible for wishing that? But Jesus, if he's alive I'm not staying. 'cause soon enough he'll know and then I'm really stuck. I have three hundred dollars in my account plus my check from work. I should leave today before Jimmy comes back . . . I could have them mail my check to wherever I end up. I'll get my clothes and junk like that and then . . . You're in an awful wreck now, Allison Johnson. You're a horrible horrible person, and you deserve what you're gonna get. You really do. You deserve it.

The man, the line cook who said he would give her a ride, was called Justin Hardgrove. She quit writing and looked up. He was standing behind the counter. She tore the paper from the small pad, crumpled it, and put it in her purse. He put out his hand and she shook it.

'It's a beater,' he said as he led her outside and towards the parking lot. 'A 1979 Eldorado. I hope you don't mind.'

'I don't even have a car,' she said.

'I guess I kind of figured,' he said. He was thirty years old with a mustache and black hair. His arms were covered in home-made tattoos. The skin on them was pocked with grease marks. He carried a paper sack.

She followed him to the car and got in the passenger side. The floor boards were filled with garbage, MD 20/20 bottles, fast food bags, used oil containers, a couple old newspapers, and brake parts.

'What part of town you need a ride to?' he asked and lit a Marlboro.

'Any part's okay. I can take the bus from wherever you stop.'

'The bus is for drunks and old ladies. I'll take you where you got to go. I just need to know where.'

'Anywhere near North Las Vegas, I guess.'

He backed the car out of the space and headed towards the highway.

'This ain't the best place to be stuck at. There's not a thing out here.'

'I know.' She looked out the window into the desert.

'Somebody kick you out of their rig?'

'Just got left here.'

'Must have gotten in a fight or something,' he said and put them on the highway.

'Kind of.'

'Why?'

'What?' she said. There were no door handles on the passenger side. She looked on the ground and saw a *Hustler* magazine underneath a Burger King bag.

'I don't like fighting.'

'I hate to fight, too,' she said uncertainly. 'I hate it more than anything.'

'Women always say that – "I hate to fight. I hate yelling." I mean no offense to you, but if you ask me it's the ladies that always do the yelling.'

'Maybe,' she said.

He reached into the paper sack that sat between him and the girl and took out a bottle of red wine he'd bought from the truck stop store.

'I never usually drink in the mornings, but with a guest I thought, what the hell, I'm gonna buy a good bottle of wine. I'm off until Wednesday night. I figured you being stuck all the way out here, you might need a drink.' He handed the bottle to her. 'I don't know if it's got a cork in it, but if it's that kind I got a corkscrew on my pocket knife that's in the glove box. Could you open it for me?'

She looked at the bottle, saw it had a cork, put the bottle

between her legs, and opened the glove box. Inside there was a roll of duct tape, extra fuses and bulbs for the car, a spool of wire. She found the pocket knife.

'You want me to open it right now?'

'No time like yesterday,' he said. He turned on the radio and pushed in a CD.

'You like music?'

'Yeah,' she said and tried to use the corkscrew. But she was beginning to get nervous. Her hands shook a little and she had trouble getting it started.

'Yeah, me too,' he said and threw his cigarette out the window and looked over at her.

'Having trouble with it?'

'I'll get it,' she said. 'The cork might fall apart, but I'll get it.'

'Don't worry, I never re-cork,' he said and laughed.

He had them in the right lane. The sun was beginning to rise across the desert. The road was nearly empty, just a few tractor-trailers, and the odd car or two passing in the other direction.

'The only good thing is the sunrise. About my job, I mean. Every morning it's like this. No traffic, no stop lights. The heat hasn't started up.'

She opened the bottle and handed it to him. She took the broken cork from the corkscrew, and put it on the dash. From the corner of her eye she could see him drink from it, and while he did, she put the pocket knife down between the passenger side door and her seat, and then she shut the glove box.

He was almost half way through the bottle when she began to hyperventilate.

'What's wrong?' he said. He slowed the car.

56

'Nothing,' she could barely say. Tears were leaking down her face.

'Are you going to have some sort of fit?'

'No."

'Are you gonna have a seizure? You want me to take you to a hospital?'

She remained silent and closed her eyes. She tried to breathe but it was hard. Her hands were balled into fists, she tried to open them but couldn't.

She began to bite the inside of her cheek, hoping it would ease her anxiety. Her heart raced so fast that she suddenly couldn't breathe, and finally she bit as hard as she could and the taste of blood filled her mouth, and with the pain and the blood she finally began to calm. She opened her fists and tried to take deep breaths. She swallowed the blood and tried to focus on Paul Newman, but it was hard to get there. The man was sitting next to her and they were in the middle of nowhere.

But she kept her eyes closed and concentrated, and then suddenly he was there. She was Paul Newman's nurse, rolling him around in a wheelchair, talking to him. He was young, not old, and it was warm out, sunny, and trees surrounded them. She was dressed in a white uniform.

He spoke to her.

'Let me tell you, when I get out of this wheelchair I'm taking you with me.'

'I bet,' she said and wheeled him towards the lawn.

'You remember when I was in *Cool Hand Luke*?'

'Of course I remember. You weren't too smart in that one.'

'If I'd met you then, I wouldn't have cut the tops off all those parking meters in the first place.'

'Did you really eat those fifty eggs?'

'Of course I did. You don't think I'm a fraud, do you?'

'Well, you sure were in *The Sting*.'

'Yeah, but that's what I'm trying to tell you, with the money I made pulling off that job, I'm loaded. That's why I'm trying to get you out of here. That's why I want you with me.'

'I thought you looked amazing in *The Sting*.'

'I still have those suits. I could wear one for you.'

'I'll have to buy new clothes then.'

'We'll go shopping once I get the hell out of this hospital.'

'So what did you really do with the money you made off that job you pulled?'

'That's what I've been trying to tell you. About twenty miles from here there's a big old house. It's near a lake. There's a pier that you can sit on. You can jump off it and go swimming. I bought that place 'cause of you. I know that's the sorta place you'd like to live in. I want us to live there together.'

'I bet.'

'I'm serious,' Paul said.

'What about snakes?'

'What do you mean?'

'In the lake, are there snakes?'

'There aren't any snakes. If you're swimming I let the snakes know it's time to take a vacation.'

'Do you promise?'

'Of course I promise. Remember me in *Where The Money Is*? I get you away from that bum husband of yours, and then I get us out of that jam, don't I?'

'You got a point there,' she said and they stopped on the lawn and looked out among the grass and the trees.

'It's a beautiful lawn, don't you think?'

'It'd be a bitch to mow, though,' he said.

'When have you ever mowed a lawn?'

'Remember *Nobody's Fool*? I mowed a lot of lawns in that one.'

'But it was winter in that one. You must have had to shovel a lot of snow to get down to the grass.'

'It's a bitch mowing the lawn in the winter. Let me tell you that. Anyway, more importantly, can you bake a pie?'

'I could learn.'

'What I'm thinking is peach pie. Peach pie and a good old cup of joe.'

'You just get me out of here and I'll bake you one a week.'

'This kid is a strange bird, I'll give you that.'

'He scares the hell out of me.'

'That shit heel boyfriend of yours. He's the one to be scared of. He sure hasn't shown much, has he?'

'No.'

'And he knocked you up.'

'I should have been more careful.'

'That would have been the best thing.'

'Why I am so pathetic?'

'You aren't. You just been dealt a rough hand, and I'm sorry to say you don't make the best decisions when you do get a break. We really got to work on your decision-making skills.'

'I want to do better.'

'Good. You know you're a good looking broad. I've never seen a girl look so good in a nurse's outfit. Those blue eyes of yours. They're something else.'

'I'm sorry I don't have much in the way of breasts.'

'Listen, when I give you a compliment you can't turn it around and hit yourself. That ain't gonna fly with me. Come to think of it, a comment like that gets me two pies a week. I might invite my old friend the Sundance Kid to share a piece. That boy can sure eat pie.'

'I'm sorry.'

'Look, first things first. Have this wine drinking pervert drop you off. A little walk wouldn't hurt you. And listen, you gotta lay off the bottle. And no caffeine. You can't drink or smoke or have caffeine. You're going to have a baby, *comprende*?"

'I'll be better.'

'You promise?'

'I promise.'

'My recommendation is to start new. Get the hell out of Dodge, as they say, and most of all, kid, buck up. This ain't the right time to cave in.'

'I'm all right,' she said finally and opened her eyes and looked out to the road passing underneath them.

The man took a drink from the bottle.

'As long as you're all right,' he said. He took the pack of cigarettes he had off the dash. 'You almost scared the shit out of me. You want a smoke?'

She wiped her eyes. 'I'm trying to quit.'

'I've quit fifteen, maybe twenty times. Longest I've lasted is seven months. Then five of my best breeding ferrets died, and I fell off the wagon. My A/C went out in the dead of the summer.'

'You breed ferrets?'

'You like them?'

'I've never seen one except in a pet store.'

'I raise them. They're a good pet. Next to a dog, I'd say a ferret is the best. A lot of people don't think so, but I know. The magazines go back and forth on it. They're good especially if you live in an apartment or duplex that don't allow dogs. They got a scent, though. A lot of people don't like that. But they love to be petted. At least mine do. Crazy thing is they're related to the wolverine, in the same family. The wolverine is a mean son of a bitch. Ferrets can get tough, but they don't usually get mean. You can teach them a lot, too. They're smart. I have forty-one right now. I usually sell off ten at a time. Sell them to a couple pet stores I know.'

'You make a lot of money?'

'Some. I just like ferrets more than anything. It takes a lot of work. More work than money.'

She found a stick of gum in her purse and put it into her mouth to kill the taste of blood.

'I've been raising them seven, almost eight years. At one time I had over ninety, but my neighbor called the Humane Society and I had to sell off most. I moved after that. But before I did I saw my neighbor smoking pot on his porch. He had a big old bong. He was growing weed in his attic. I called the cops, which I hated doing, but people should mind their own goddamn business.'

She could see the outskirts of the city in the distance. The sun was up now, moving across the sky. They came to a suburb and stopped at a light. He put them in the right lane and turned onto a side street.

'Where we going?' she asked.

'I just got to make a quick stop.'

'You can drop me off here then.'

'Listen,' he said, 'you're still ten miles from where you want to be. You don't want to be stuck on the bus all day, do you? I'll only be a minute.'

'Okay,' she said finally. 'But then you'll take me into town?'

'I told you I would,' he said and worked his way through side streets until he came to a large lot with an old yellow double wide trailer parked in the center. There was a dying cottonwood tree behind it, with its broken and dry branches hanging limply over the trailer's roof trying to give it cover. There was a small patch of grass near the front door circled in chicken wire.

'This is my place,' he said and pulled into the drive and parked the car. 'It ain't much but what are you going to do?'

He found a pair of vise grips on the floor boards and handed them to her. 'You got to use them to get out. These cars are pieces of shit, all the handles broke off in the same year. You can come in if you want.'

'I'll just sit in the car,' she said.

'Suit yourself,' he said and got out and disappeared inside.

He came out of his trailer a half hour later dressed in black pants and a pink short-sleeve dress shirt. He'd showered and shaved. He was carrying a small cage with a ferret inside and a paper sack. He walked to the car, opened the driver's side door, and put the cage and the sack in the back seat. He got in, shut the door, started the engine, and backed onto the street.

He lit a cigarette. The stereo was still playing and he began to sing along with the song in a quiet, broken voice. When it ended, he took a drink off the nearly empty wine bottle, looked at her, and said, 'What do you think of her?'

'Who?'

'The ferret.'

'I don't know,' the girl said. 'I didn't really notice her.'

He gave a faint whistle. 'Come to me, little Emily,' he said. 'Come here to me, little one. Show this lady your stuff.'

He called again as he drove, this time in a louder voice. The ferret began making noises and pacing back and forth in the cage.

'What's she doing?' the girl asked. She turned around in her seat and looked at the animal moving about in its cage. 'She's running around so fast. Is she upset?'

'Come on, Emily,' he said again. 'Come on, little one.'

He kept talking to her. The same thing over and over. The ferret began pacing quicker, its noises grew louder. The girl sat back and faced the road ahead of them.

'There's nothing to be scared of. She's harmless,' he said and laughed. 'We're just playing.'

He got them back on the main road.

The girl heard noises in the back and turned around again only to see the cage and the small latch door on it open. The ferret wasn't there, but she could hear it wandering around the floor below her making its way through the magazines and papers and bottles.

'She's gotten out, I think.'

'Has she?' he said and turned off the music. He looked in the rearview. 'Did you get out? Jesus, Emily's good if she did that.'

'She's out,' the girl said nervously.

The man pushed up the speed of the Eldorado, and moved them into the left lane.

The girl got more worried and grabbed the pocket knife that lay between the seat and the door and opened a blade. She lifted her legs up onto the seat.

'Could you pull over?' she said finally. 'I'm sorry, but that thing scares me. I can walk from here.'

Justin eased off on the gas, moved into the right lane. 'Hell, I was going to see if you wanted to keep her. She's my favorite one.'

'I'm sorry,' the girl said, her voice cracking in fear.

'Emily,' he said. 'Come here, little one.'

The ferret moved slowly underneath the seat and climbed up and moved to between his legs. He pulled the car off the road and onto the shoulder. She set the pocket knife on the floor, and with the vise grips opened the door and got out. She didn't say anything at all. She just walked away from the car as fast as she could.

He sat there in his car for a long time, holding the ferret and watching the endless rows of cars pass him. He could feel his depression slowly creeping back in, just with that ride, just with seeing the way the girl almost cried. His eyes began to water, he took a drink off the wine bottle, then looked in his rearview for a space, and got back on the road.

THE LAMPLIGHTER

The girl walked two blocks before she stopped on the shoulder of the road to look back and make sure he was gone. A clock on the bank across the street read nine-thirty. It was too late to go to work. In her purse she found another stick of gum. She figured she was only half a mile from the Lamplighter, so she'd go there, get a drink, and figure out what to do.

She made the walk there, and inside ordered a vodka and 7UP. She looked through her purse, found a pen and the new pad of paper, and when the bartender sat her drink down, she finished it in three swallows, and began to write names of cities on the paper. Seattle, Portland, San Francisco, Boise, Houston, Reno. She wrote their names over and over, each time with more uncertainty.

She ordered another drink and went to the bathroom. When she came back, she finished that drink, then looked in her purse, and counted her money. She ordered another and lit a cigarette. She'd calm down first. Calm down as much as the $17.50 in her wallet would let her, and then she'd decide where to go.

LEAVING

She was drunk when she closed her bank account, and drunk when she got on the city bus to her mother's house. Sweat dripped from her face as she sat on the plastic bus seat. She stared out the window and the city passed before her. With each building she passed, she was more certain.

She got off at her regular stop and walked to her house, opened the chain link fence by the garage, and walked into the backyard. The Hulk was laying under the picnic table, and she bent down to pet him, then unlocked the back door, and led him inside. She turned the A/C on high, took off her clothes, went into the bathroom, and took a shower.

She dressed, then found her mom's old suitcase. She threw her clothes inside, along with her Patti Page and Brenda Lee tapes. Her framed picture of Paul Newman she wrapped in an old sweater and surrounded it with clothes. She went to the bathroom and took her toiletries out. Then she cooked hamburgers from some frozen patties in the freezer for the dog and her.

When she'd eaten and done the dishes, she went through the yellow pages and found the pregnancy crisis hotline and dialed the number.

'I just turned twenty-two and I'm pregnant,' she told the woman who answered. 'I've taken four home tests. I'm almost three months now. I'm gonna go to Reno to have it, and I want to give it up for adoption. I need, if you have them, the numbers for any

66

places there that can help me.'

'There are a few good places in Reno where I can direct you. Have you heard of Casa De Vida? I'll give you their number. Are you in Las Vegas now?'

'Yes.'

'Do you have family to help you in Reno?'

'No. I have no family anywhere.'

'No one at all?' the woman asked.

'My grandparents, the Watsons, used to live near Reno in a town called Verdi, but they're dead now. I have about three hundred dollars. I could get a job for a while, then I don't know what I'll do.'

'There's a lot of adoption agencies that can help with expenses. Do you have insurance?'

'No,' the girl said and tears began to fill her eyes.

'Remember there are people who can help. I think St Mary's Hospital in Reno also has a program set up specifically for women in situations like yours. Adoption agencies can often help, too. The prospective parents will sometimes pay for you to have a decent place to stay if you can't work and don't have any family help. I know it's hard, but try to relax, you're going to be okay. We'll find people who can help you.'

'Thank you,' she said and wiped her eyes.

The woman paused, then came back with the numbers and addresses, and the girl wrote them on a small pad her mother kept by the phone.

'When you get to Reno, if you have any questions you can contact the pregnancy center there or you can contact me – I'm Nancy Collins. Will you please do that? There's good places up there, and they'll have counselors who can talk to you about your different options.'

'Thank you, I'll call them,' the girl said and hung up.

She'd phone her mom once she got to the bus station and tell her not to tell anyone where she was going. Not even Evelyn. Then she called a cab and wrote a quick note on the back of an envelope,

> Mom and Evelyn,
> Had to leave for a while, don't worry. I'll call and tell you what's going on. Don't call Jimmy. And if he calls just tell him you don't know where I am, that I just left. I'm leaving 'cause of him. I'm sorry and I love you both,
> Allison

She put the note on the kitchen table, hugged the dog, and left the house. She sat on her suitcase on the sidewalk and waited for the cab. When it came, the driver put her suitcase in the trunk and she got in the back seat and he drove out of her neighborhood.

'I need to go to the bus station,' she told the driver.

'Where you going to?' he asked.

'Nowhere, I don't think.'

OXBOW MOTEL

When the bus stopped in Reno it was nighttime, near three a.m., and she sat in the rundown bus station not knowing where to go. The other passengers disappeared and the terminal emptied, and when it did she saw the driver of her bus heading towards a back room and she asked if he knew where the casinos were. He pointed in a general direction and she picked up her suitcase and left.

She could see street lights in the distance and a few cars passed on what seemed like a main road. She walked in the darkness towards it. She could hear the sound of a river, and as she walked closer to it and the main street, she saw the lights from the casinos. The Comstock marquee appeared, then the Sundowner, and the Sands shone in the distance by itself. She made her way to Virginia Street, the main strip the casinos lined. There were people streaming in and out of the clubs. She walked past the Virginian and the Cal Neva and Harrah's. There were pawn shops and souvenir stores, and she passed them and finally saw a motel called the Oxbow. A small yellow building with an ox, in neon, on the side.

The front desk clerk was an old Indian man who spoke poor English. He told her a weekly room was $150. She filled out the card and paid him in cash. He gave her the key and she carried her suitcase up to the room, locked the door behind her, put a chair underneath the knob, and sat on the bed and cried.

The room had a double bed, a desk, a dresser, a TV, and a bath-room. She'd never been in a motel room by herself, let alone in a city. She'd barely even left Las Vegas and now she'd done so by herself. The crying wouldn't stop. She shut off the lights in the room and got in bed still wearing her clothes. Pictures of Jimmy appeared in her mind. The time he had gotten them a suite at Caesars, or when they'd go swimming in the lake. Times when he was decent to her, when he was kind. In the darkness she found the phone. It sat on a bedside table and she held it. She wanted to call him, to give in, but she also hated herself for wanting to so badly.

As the night wore on, her anxieties worsened. She couldn't sleep. Her body shook. She wanted to die. To disappear. To have the cleaning lady come in and find nothing, not a trace that she had ever been there. Not a trace she'd ever been anywhere or done anything in the world.

THREE MONTHS

The next morning she woke early and walked up and down the small strip of casinos which littered downtown. From a payphone she called her mother and told her she'd left for good, that she'd gone to Reno to get away from Jimmy Bodie.

Her mother didn't understand why she'd leave town, why she'd go to Reno of all places. The girl tried to explain it, and finally told her mother of a time when he had locked her in the trunk of his car. She had passed out at a party only to awaken in the darkness of a trunk. He left her in there overnight. In the parking lot across the street from his apartment.

Her mother began crying.

'Let me come get you,' she said.

'I can't go back there,' the girl said.

'Where are you staying? You can at least tell me that.'

'I gotta go,' she said and hung up the phone. Then she went through her purse, found the note with the number of the local pregnancy resource center, and called them for directions.

It was located in a rundown strip mall. In an office. Two middle aged women sat inside behind a partition. The girl introduced herself and the older of the two ladies took her into a back room with two chairs, a small coffee table, and Christian posters on the wall. The woman gave her a glass of water, and the girl told the woman her story.

'I don't know who the father is,' she told the lady. 'I used to drink a lot. It happened at a fraternity party when I was in college. I can't remember who it was.' Adoption was what she wanted. She tried not to cry, but she broke down more than once. The woman was patient and hugged the girl and kept her talking. She would only interrupt to say things like, 'The child's welfare is the most important thing. It's good that you're here. I can help you, I can help your baby.'

The woman called two adoption agencies. She set up times for meetings. The girl took another pregnancy test and confirmed her situation, and by the end of the second week they had decided on an adoption agency, a doctor, and had seen folders of prospective parents. It was weeks after that that they finally decided on a couple that both she and the woman thought were the best. She met with the couple just once. They all sat around a table. The girl remained silent while the couple talked to her. They told her about themselves, about what sort of life they would give the baby, what sort of house the baby would live in, what sort of extended family they had.

The couple paid for medical coverage through St Mary's hospital. They arranged prenatal care and prenatal classes. The couple gave the girl a fifteen hundred dollar a month stipend and she moved into a prepaid quad with three other pregnant girls.

The apartment complex was near St Mary's, on Fifth Street, downtown. It had a large communal kitchen and two bathrooms. Her private bedroom came furnished with a separate entrance, and another lockable door that led into the kitchen area. There was a TV, a single bed and dresser, an alarm clock, and a sink.

The other girls were in various stages of the same situation. At times they would sit at the kitchen table and tell their stories. When asked, the girl left out Jimmy Bodie, her mother, her sister Evelyn, even Las Vegas, and when asked, only said, 'All I know is that if my father found out he'd kill me. He really would.'

At night, when she couldn't sleep, she'd watch TV or listen to her tapes. She wouldn't write anything down, and hadn't since she had left Las Vegas. The other girls would see movies, watch TV together, go shopping, but she never felt comfortable enough around them, and most days she just sat in her room or took long walks through the city. During her fourth month she got a job as a lunch waitress at the Cal Neva Casino. She worked three days a week, and began to sleep better once the job started. She opened a bank account and deposited each month's stipend and used her tips for food money.

In the middle of her eighth month she was no longer able to work and spent most of her time going to the library or watching TV. She'd never read much, but met a librarian and asked the woman if she knew where she could get a high school reading list.

The librarian made a list for her and the girl began checking out books. One by one she read *Beloved* by Toni Morrison, *Ethan Frome* by Edith Wharton. She read John Steinbeck and Ernest Hemingway. Pearl S. Buck and Charles Dickens, Nathaniel Hawthorne and Walter Van Tilburg Clark.

Throughout the months, though, her anxiety never eased or slowed down. She had hoped being away from Jimmy would somehow calm her nerves, but they continued as they always had. Most of all she was frightened that her nervousness would affect the baby. Each time she felt a panic attack coming, with her body shaking, her breath shortening, she would break down and cry, scared that somehow it would cause the baby to abort or cause some sort of unseen damage.

Oftentimes in the middle of the night she would lay awake and think about the baby. She felt it was a boy and in her mind thought of him as such. She wondered what he would look like, and what he would become. If he would be a good person. In her heart, she didn't want to give him away, and some nights she would pray over and over that Jimmy Bodie would be killed before the baby came, and she could then, finally, keep him.

The few times she called her mother she asked about him, hoping that somehow he was finished. That he'd gotten in a car wreck, or maybe gotten killed in a fight or died in a fire. But her mother would always reply that he had called a few days earlier or had just left a message on the machine.

As the weeks of her ninth month passed she spent more time in bed and more time sleeping. And then near dawn one morning, she had pain in her guts. She walked into the kitchen and knocked on another pregnant girl's door and told her that she wasn't positive, but that she was pretty sure it was her time.

The other girl had a car and drove her to St Mary's and sat with her until a nurse came and put her in a room. Then the other pregnant girl disappeared, and she had the baby alone. Only the nurses and the doctor were present, and her labor was long, but by dusk she had a son.

The adopting couple were led into the room moments after the birth. Allison began crying at the sight of them. The nurse held the baby and she left the room with him and the new family. Allison fell asleep in exhaustion.

Hours later, when she woke, she tried to get up and leave. A nurse came in and stopped her and talked to her. It was the middle of the night. The nurse opened the blinds and the girl stared out the window at the city lights and wished she was dead. There was a show playing on the TV but she could only vaguely hear it. It felt miles away, like she was disappearing down a long hole. She thought of her son and her heart began to race. Her breath shortened and tears filled her eyes, but as the panic got more intense exhaustion took over, and she closed her eyes and once again fell asleep.

Two weeks later she moved out of the quad. She had six thousand dollars saved in a bank account and over a thousand dollars cash in her purse. She had hoped to move again, to put Reno and what had happened there behind her. For days she went to the bus station staring at the rows of destinations they had posted, but in the end she knew she could never leave. She felt she had to be in the same city as her baby even if she could never see him. So when the last day at the quad came, she put her two suitcases in storage at the bus station and went to look for an apartment.

She walked past downtown and headed east on Fourth Street. She stopped at the first apartment building that had a 'For rent' sign and went to the manager's door. It was called the Emerald Arms. It was a mid-1950s two-story apartment complex with ten units. It had been in a state of ill repair for the last fifteen years, and its quality of tenants had fallen along with it.

The room wasn't much, just a second story studio apartment. It was a decent sized room with stained tan carpet, an old table and two chairs, a kitchenette, and a twin bed. The place smelled of cigar and cigarette smoke and the once white walls were faded and yellow from it.

The manager stared out the window while she looked it over. He was a middle-aged Greek man who spoke with a thick accent. He was overweight and dressed in faded, worn out gray sweats. His gut hung out over the waistband and she could see his hairy skin from there. He looked like he hadn't shaved or showered in days and she could smell him from where she stood. She walked into the bathroom where there was an old full size tub, a sink, and toilet. The paint on the walls was bubbled, and loose linoleum sat on top of nearly rotten floor boards. There was mildew on the bath and sink and it all smelled of urine.

'I'm not going to pay for a cleaning deposit,' the girl said as strongly as she could. 'I'll take the place, but it hasn't been cleaned. I can barely go into the bathroom it smells so bad.'

'It's been cleaned,' the landlord said and turned to her.

'I don't think so,' she said and walked to the kitchen area. There was a half size refrigerator, a sink, and a kitchen table and stove. She opened the refrigerator. Inside was a package of rotten hamburger, a carton of milk, condiments, and a few Chinese take out boxes.

'Did you clean this out, too?'

He walked over and coughed when the odor came to him.

'Let me plug it back in. At least we can try to freeze the smell.'

He found the plug and put it into the wall socket.

'Look,' he said, 'I'll cut out the cleaning deposit and knock half the rent off the first month if you take it the way it is, today. That's my offer, take it or leave it.'

'All utilities are paid?'

'Yes,' he said and coughed again.

'It's three hundred dollars a month?'

The man nodded.

'You can have a phone here?'

'There's a wall jack.'

'I'll take it then,' she said and opened her purse. She took out seven hundred and fifty dollars and handed it to him. 'This is for three months then. I'll need a receipt.'

'Good,' the landlord said and took the money and left the room. He came back minutes later with a handwritten receipt and the keys. 'There's a dumpster', he said, 'behind the building. It's for all the tenants to use. You might want to start at the fridge. I also have a newer mattress in the storage room. If you want it let me know.'

'I guess I'll take the newer one then,' she said, smiling, and the man nodded.

The girl followed him out and walked down to the bus station where she'd left her things and took a cab back to the apartment. The new bed was there when she entered the room, the old one sitting outside leaned against the wall. She dropped her things inside, then went back to the cab she'd kept waiting, and told the driver to take her to a K-Mart. There she bought new sheets for the bed, a couple of bath towels, three gallons of white paint, a roller and brush. She also bought a reading lamp, cleaning supplies, and a set of pots and pans.

She called another cab from the store and the driver took her back to the Emerald Arms. She left the packages on the floor, then left again and walked down Fourth Street to the Salvation Army. She bought a few plates, glasses, and utensils. She bought a blanket and a faded comforter. There was an old radio from the 1960s, and she took that as well. On the way back she stopped at a liquor store, bought a six pack of beer, a bottle of water, and *People* magazine.

She emptied the refrigerator first, then plugged in the radio and set it on the kitchen table. She found a country station, put on a pair of rubber gloves, filled the sink with hot water and soap, and began to clean. She started with the kitchen and refrigerator. She wiped down the counter and the cabinets. She sprayed down the fridge, then put the beer and a box of baking soda inside it. She scrubbed the floors.

The bathroom she sprayed down with disinfectant and scrubbed it clean. She put her towels on a rack, and put her toiletries in the mirrored cabinet. It was almost evening by then and she began to feel weak, and she stopped and took a beer from the fridge and opened it. She sat at the table and began thumbing through *People* magazine.

When she felt rested enough, she washed and put away her new cookware. She borrowed a vacuum from the landlord, ran it over the carpet, and returned it to him. Then she called another cab and had the driver take her to a grocery store where she bought a hundred dollars worth of food and called another cab to take her home.

When the last of the grocery bags had been brought in she locked the door behind her and put a chair underneath the knob. She put the new sheets, the blanket, and the comforter on the bed, but it was her first night completely alone and she was uneasy. She went to the refrigerator and took out a beer and opened it. She turned on the radio again and sat at the kitchen table. She'd have to get a TV, something to take up time at night.

She drank the beer quickly and opened another. She could hear her neighbors, the faint sound of a TV, of people talking, of running water. She'd get a phone tomorrow and then find a job. She wanted to take a bath, but didn't feel like taking off her clothes and laying naked in a room she was nervous in. What if the old tenants came back? What if they still had the keys? What if the landlord walked in, what if some old tenant broke in? She'd have to get a new lock tomorrow and told herself she'd hook up a chain as well.

The station on the radio faded in and out and finally she turned it off. In the quiet she drank another beer, then found her cigarettes, lit one, and then thoughts of her baby came to her. What were they doing right then? Were they all sleeping in the same room? Maybe the baby was asleep in a crib and the couple were in a bed next to him quietly talking to each other. Maybe the baby was up crying and the woman was holding him and watching TV. Maybe she was dressed in a robe, in a nice house with a big yard and a deck.

The girl sat at the table and cried. She hated herself for giving her baby away. For being weak, for running and now for being alone. Horrible thoughts about herself came to her and once they did, they wouldn't leave. She began to panic, her breath grew short, and she hyperventilated.

'You're horrible,' she repeated over to herself. 'You're the most horrible person in the world.'

She could hardly sit still, her whole body shook. She took the cigarette from the ashtray, took pulls from it until it was red hot, then lifted the sleeve on her shirt and on her bicep, next to the other scars, she put the cigarette out.

The pain eased her anxiety as it always did. Her breath returned and her body relaxed. She put the cigarette in the tray and blew cool air on the burn. She finished her beer and went to the fridge for another and kept drinking until she was drunk. Then she took the comforter off the bed, found her walkman and her purse, and went into the bathroom. She locked the door behind her, found in her purse her father's old pocket knife, and opened it to the longest blade.

In the darkness, sitting on the cold linoleum floor, the girl kept beating herself up. Her thoughts became darker and darker as time passed, and they ended at the bottom where they always did: with the memories of the busboys at the Horseshoe Casino.

There were two of them. Mexicans who could barely speak English. They would say things to her in Spanish that she couldn't understand. They would whistle, the older one would sometimes pinch her and grab at her butt. She told the older waitresses and they told her to tell the manager and to stand up for herself, to say something.

But she didn't say anything.

One evening the older busboy grabbed her breast and hurt her. She had been in the back, in the store room, getting a plastic gallon jug of maple syrup. The dinner rush was over and she was restocking. He followed her. He said things to her, grabbed at her. She threw the jug at him and hit him in the face with it. He fell to the ground. She screamed. The head cook came. The busboy stood and began yelling at her in Spanish. The head cook began yelling at the busboy in Spanish. The girl told the cook what he had done. The cook grabbed the busboy by the shirt and began pushing him back against the freezer. Another cook came back and broke it up.

The cap to the jug had broken and syrup leaked over the floor. The head cook pointed to it and yelled at the busboy in Spanish, and the busboy slowly began to clean it up. He also apologized to the girl for the busboy, who was his cousin. He was new, the cook said, and he admitted he didn't know him very well, but assured her that it wouldn't happen again.

That evening, after her shift, she sat in the bar nearest the restaurant and had a drink with one of the other waitresses.

'They're not all like that, but a lot are,' her co-worker said. The woman was forty-five and had three kids. She'd been a waitress since age fourteen. She was drinking a gin and 7UP, playing video poker. 'It's 'cause you're young and cute. If you weren't cute, if you were fat and old with a bunch of kids like me then they'd leave you alone.' The woman laughed and finished her drink. 'You got to be tougher. Those boys don't like that. Tell them you got a husband who's a cop. It seems stupid but it works, believe me. Wear a wedding ring. My husband thinks it's 'cause they're all raised Catholic and their girls don't give it up easily, except for the prostitutes. So then when they see American movies and American girls having sex all the time they look at you thinking you're like that, that you're a real slut. You should hear the shit they say amongst themselves. At least José was there. He's a good guy, he's just trying to get his relatives jobs, but you can't choose your relatives, can you?'

'The thing that drives me crazy', Allison whispered, 'is that when I talk to the busboys and ask them to do something, like clear a table or whatever, they act like they don't understand a word of English. I have to explain it to them over and over. I have to walk out to the table and show them. But then other times when you just say something to them, something unrelated to work, like, did you have a nice weekend? Or, how's your baby, or whatever, then they understand you and answer you.'

The woman laughed again. 'Yeah, I never thought of that but that's true. The key is don't talk to them. Don't pay any attention to them. Make friends with one of the cooks, one of the in-charge guys. That's what I always do. The Mexicans don't want any real trouble. If they know you got people who could get them fired, then they won't do it, and they won't ever bother you again.'

The two women continued talking until the older waitress's husband came to pick her up. Allison had two more beers by herself and then left. It was winter and the air was cold. She could see her breath as she left the casino. She walked down the street towards her mom's car. She was drunk. She was wearing a coat and had a scarf around her neck. It was late out and there was no traffic passing when she turned down the side street, near the alley where she always parked.

The next thing she knew she was on her back and the older busboy from the restaurant was punching her in the stomach. The younger one held her arms. She screamed at first, and then when she saw who they were, she froze. She was sure they would kill her. She started to hyperventilate, she lost her wind and almost blacked out. The older busboy, the one on top of her, pulled up her skirt and ripped her underwear from her. He undid his pants and entered her. She began crying as he moved back and forth. He said things to her in Spanish that she couldn't understand. He spat on her. She looked at the younger one, the one holding her arms. She looked at him in the eyes, and when she did, he looked back and let go. He yelled at the older busboy and stood up. He pulled the other man off her and they both went running.

She lay there on the cold street. She stared at the sky, the stars overhead. She couldn't breathe. She heard a car drive by, saw the beeping lights of an airplane overhead. She could feel her legs and rear on the frost-covered street, and the scarf still around her neck. Then suddenly her breath released from her mouth, disappeared into the sky, and she could breathe again.

She stood up slowly and walked to the car and drove home. Once inside her mother's house, she took off her clothes, took a shower, put on a nightgown, and sat in front of the TV. She didn't go to work the next day or the day after that. She didn't answer the phone or collect her last check. She stayed in for three weeks sleeping on the couch, leaving only to go to the grocery store. She didn't tell anyone about it, not her mother, not her sister. Her mother worked nights and had a new boyfriend. She spent most of her off hours with him, and by the time she did ask Allison about her life, the girl had started another waitressing job at the Plaza.

When she woke the next morning she was on the bathroom floor. She was hung over and sick to her stomach. She got up, put the comforter back on the bed, got a glass of water, took three aspirin, and started the tub. It was early out, six o'clock, and the sun was just hitting her room.

She grabbed her walkman, undressed, and got in the tub. She started the tape player. Patti Page came on the headphones. She had only two tapes. Patti Page and Brenda Lee. She closed her eyes and tried to figure out what to do. She would keep herself busy and try not to think about the past anymore. She would get her job back at the Cal Neva and then try to find something else, a job to get out of waitressing. Maybe she'd work in a store, she knew how to use a cash register, knew how to give change. She could answer phones, she had a driver's license.

Her thoughts began to race as she thought of her uncertain future. Her anxieties started again. Her breaths quickened and her body tensed. She pinched her leg as hard as she could, hoping that would stop it. She closed her eyes and thought of Paul Newman. She focused on his face and his blue eyes.

'So, kid, how's the water?'

'At least the water heater's good,' she said.

'This place ain't much, but I think you'll do all right.' He was sitting beside her on the toilet, drinking a beer.

'You sure do like Budweiser.'

'It's the king of beers.'

'I'm a terrible person. I don't know why you ever talk to me.'

'We all have tough times. Remember me in *The Verdict*. I was drunk as a bum for more than twenty years in that one.'

'But you were a lawyer, you'd gone to college.'

'Listen, kid, you could go to college. Believe me, you're smart enough.'

'You think so?'

'I'm sure of it.'

'I've done some horrible things.'

'We all have. You ever seen *Hud*?'

'You sure were an asshole in that one.'

'I've been bad. You aren't bad. You just got what I'd call bad nerves. That, my girl, you're gonna have to work on. We got to toughen you up. That's why you're in the boat you're in.'

'I just wish we could disappear together.'

'We do all the time.'

'Remember when you were in *Hombre*? I would have taken care of you in that one. I would have had us sneak away and get a place a thousand miles from anywhere.'

'They sure were rough on me in that one. Indians don't get many breaks.'

'I wouldn't have let you go down the hill and get shot. I would have gone down myself.'

'I know you would have, kid. That's why I'm here.'

'You think he's gonna be all right? Do you think they'll be all right to him?'

'I just stopped by this morning. His new dad is a hell of a good guy. That's something to know. You shouldn't worry. You did the right thing.'

'What are they like?'

'They stayed up all night worrying about him. They got a hell of a nice house, too. Plus his new mom is the most patient gal in the world. I sure as hell wish I was as good a parent as they're gonna be.'

'You promise they're that way?'

'Of course I promise.'

'What are they doing right now?'

'Sleeping, which is what you should be doing.'

'I feel horrible.'

'I'd make you breakfast if I could. I can cook like a son of a bitch. I know how to make a breakfast that'll cure any hangover.'

'I really like your spaghetti sauce.'

'That's just the tip of the iceberg, kid.'

'You know something that doesn't make sense?'

'What's that?'

'My sister Evelyn likes Robert Redford better in *Butch Cassidy and the Sundance Kid*. I can't believe she'd say something like that.'

'She's just a kid, what do you expect?'

'You won't leave me, will you?'

'Look, if I wasn't so old I'd jump right in there with you. You're a hell of a catch.'

'I bet.'

'You are. I told old Bob Redford about you, and he's jealous as hell.'

'You're the only one I like.'

'I know, kid. You're a real gem that way. Now get out of the tub, it's time to give it another try.'

'All right,' she said.

'And kid—'

'Yeah?'

'Buy a TV, you think too much.'

CAL NEVA

The Cal Neva Top Deck restaurant re-hired her and when they did, she asked to be put on graveyard shift. She was scared to sleep at night in the apartment alone, and the restaurant even at that late hour was half full and the tips decent. The drunks were there, but a security guard and a manager walked the floor and together they made sure the customers stayed in line.

At the end of the first month she had regulars, and the regulars became the first friends she had in town. There was a frail old woman who dressed in western outfits. She wore a scarf around her neck and cowboy boots. Her teeth were either missing or rotten. She was a drunk. Every night at two a.m. she came in, sat in the girls' section, and ordered the late night Calorie Saver Special: a single hamburger patty, cottage cheese, a half peach in light syrup, and wheat toast. She never ate the hamburger, just had it put in a to-go bag.

'Saving it for later?' the girl asked her one night.

'I have a dog named Cottonball. It's his only supper.'

'What about you?'

'Me?'

'Is this your only supper?'

'It is,' the old woman whispered. 'How did you know?'

'Just a guess,' the girl said. 'If I give you an extra patty to go, will you eat the one on the plate?'

'I don't have the money.'

'I do,' the girl said.

The woman nodded, and so the girl began giving her an extra hamburger patty each time she came in, taking it out of her tip money.

A little while later the old lady began leaving drink tokens and old horse racing magazines in return. She left snapshots of the dog, old blank postcards, and even a copy of an old Brenda Lee record after the girl told her she was her favorite singer.

Most nights just after her shift started a middle-aged black man came in alone, sat in her section, and ordered a chicken fried steak, mashed potatoes with vegetables, a side order of bacon, extra gravy, and three biscuits. He always dressed well, in slacks and a sweater or in a suit. He wore thick bifocal glasses. His hair was black and gray and there was a saucer-sized bald spot on the crown of his head. He wore a black leather coat and black leather shoes and sat with a stack of sports papers and marked them with different colored pens he had lined up in a row on the table.

'So you're a gambler?' the girl asked.

'I try not to look at it as gambling,' he said and laughed.

'Do you want me to see if I can get you a pitcher of coffee?'

'I drink that much?' he said.

'It seems like you can drink a lot. Every time I pass by your cup's empty,' she said and pointed to the Thermos sitting beside him.

'Looks like that fella has been stealing it.'

'It does,' the girl said and smiled.

'You caught me,' he said and put his hands up in the air.

'Do you stay up all night?'

'I hate sleeping at night. I've always slept from sunrise to eleven a.m.'

'Give me the Thermos,' she said and he handed it to her and she filled it to the top with the pot she was carrying. 'Just don't tell anyone.'

'Look it here. In exchange I'm going to give you a sure win on a pick four.' He took a pen and a Post-it Note and wrote down a series of football team names. 'This is for Sunday. All you got to do is go to the sports book and tell the man behind the counter "pick four" and then list all the names I gave you as the winners and put a twenty on it, and I swear Christmas will come early.'

He handed the note to her and she put it in her apron.

'Can I ask you one other question?'

'You name it,' he said.

'How can you eat so much and be so skinny?'

'This is the only meal I eat a day. Plus my mother was as skinny as a piece of wire.'

'I hope I'm always like that.'

'Looks to me like you could eat an entire buffet and come out the other end a bit on the thin side,' he said and grinned.

The next evening she filled his Thermos and all the nights afterward. The man brought in his wife every Thursday and they sat on the same side of the table. They filled out Keno tickets, drank cocktails, and ate. The wife always tripled the tip and told the girl her husband thought she was a good luck charm.

There was another man, in his late twenties, who was there each morning at five-fifteen, forty-five minutes before her shift ended. He ordered the ninety-nine cent breakfast, eggs different each day, always bacon, always sourdough toast, a glass of water, and coffee with cream. On Fridays he ordered steak and eggs and a tall glass of orange juice.

He sat alone and each morning he wore the same thing: black work shoes and a dark blue uniform with a patch on the left breast that read 'Dan'. He had brown eyes, short brown hair, and a clean shaven face. He was built thin and was small boned. On his face was a scar that ran from the outside edge of his right eye down to the middle of his cheek. The scar was thin but the color was darker than his flesh. His right eyelid lay lazy over half the eye. She noticed the eye moving, watching her as she delivered his food, and she thought that it must work, at least partially.

It was on a Friday morning that she noticed him earlier, at five a.m. He was reading the newspaper and was dressed in his own clothes. A red flannel shirt and jeans. When he sat down a cocktail waitress passed him and he placed an order.

'Good morning,' the girl said and smiled when she came to his table.

'Hello,' he said, looked at her, and smiled back.

'I don't think I've seen you in normal clothes before.'

'I took the day off. My uncle and me are heading down to San Francisco to watch the horse races at Bay Meadows.'

'I've never been to San Francisco,' she said. 'The Golden Gate Bridge, it's there, right?'

'Yeah and it's nice, too. You can walk across it if you want. San Francisco is a good place. It's got a ton of people, but the buildings are beautiful. Plus they have horse races. I don't bet well, but I like them all right. Afterwards my uncle and me go to Chinatown or little Italy and eat and then stay the night at a motel in

93

Chinatown, and then we come back in the morning.'

'Where do you work?' she asked.

'The VA Hospital. You haven't worked here long, have you?' he asked.

'No,' she said. 'I just moved here.'

'Where from?'

'San Diego,' she said.

'My uncle, the same one I mentioned, he and I been down there a few times. For car shows and things like that.'

'They have a lot of things like that.'

'Seems like it,' he said.

The cocktail waitress came with a Heineken and a screwdriver. He paid her, tipped her, and the woman walked away.

'I should take your order,' she said.

'I almost forgot,' he said and took a drink from his beer. 'I'll have the steak special and medium on the steak.'

'Scrambled eggs, sourdough toast, and hash browns?'

'Yeah. That's it. I know I'm pretty boring to always eat the same thing. At least today I'm a little different,' he said, embarrassed.

'I eat the same thing every morning. It's good to, I think,' she said and began to write his order down.

'Do you like Reno?' he asked when she finished.

'What I've seen of it, I do. I like the weather. I'm excited for the cold, and to see snow when winter comes. San Diego is always the same. Once in a while it gets cold, but it's not that different. I've never really been where there's snow on the ground. I'd like to buy a winter coat and really wear it, you know?'

'Yeah,' he said and took another drink off his beer.

'Okay, we're all set,' she said and walked away.

94

She put his order into the computer, grabbed a fresh pot of coffee, and hit her tables. Then she delivered his food and filled up his coffee once more. By then, though, she had three new tables, and the next time she passed where he had sat, he was gone.

The drinks were empty, but the food was nearly untouched. There was a five dollars tip on the table, and on a bar napkin he'd written, 'I'll bet a horse for you,' in black Keno crayon.

After her shift she changed in the employee bathroom and walked down to the river and drank a cup of coffee. She had found a pack of Pall Malls on a table that morning, and picked it up and put it in her apron. She took a cigarette from the pack and lit it.

The sun was coming up over the mountains and beginning to lay down upon the city. Every morning for the last three weeks she'd left work and taken a walk. She knew she couldn't spend too much time alone in her apartment. When she did, her thoughts caught her. But that morning she was too tired to walk and decided to give up and buy a TV.

She finished her coffee and cigarette and headed down Virginia Street until she saw, in the distance, an electronics store. She sat in front of the building until it opened, then went inside and bought a nineteen inch color TV. She had the store call a cab and she waited outside until the taxi came and drove her back to the apartment.

She carried the TV with her to her mailbox. It was on the ground floor, near the manager's room. Inside it was a bill from the telephone company and a large manila envelope from her mother. She put the mail in her purse, picked up the TV, and carried it up into her room. Once inside, she took it from the box, set it on a chair, and plugged it in.

She found three stations that came in. She undressed, brushed her teeth, and got in bed with the manila envelope. Inside was a note from her mother, a twenty-dollar bill, two snapshots of Evelyn and Junior in Mexico, and a letter. The letter was addressed to her from Jimmy Bodie. Her mother, in her note, wrote that he had been by once a week since she'd left. She said that he looked like a beat-up horse, and that all he did was talk about how much he missed the girl. So she finally broke down and told him to write a letter and if he did, she would include it in a package she was sending.

Allison put the note back in the envelope, and looked at the pictures of Evelyn and Junior. In one of them they were on the beach and it was near sunset and they were both tanned and waving at the camera. The second was of Evelyn standing in front of Junior's uncle's van. It was parked alongside a city street in a Mexican town. There were shop signs in Spanish above them, and Evelyn was leaning against the old van wearing a sombrero. She stared at the photographs, and then got up and taped them to the wall next to the bed. She changed the channel on the TV, laid back down, and opened the letter from Jimmy.

Allison,

I don't know if your mom will even give you this letter, but if she does, you got to let me have your address and phone number. She already let it slip that you lived in Reno. Why the hell would you move up there? There ain't much to it if I remember right. I have a cousin who lives in Fernley and we used to visit him there and then stay in Reno for a couple days. What a shit hole that place is. But I've been meaning to visit him and when I do I'll come up and visit you, too. Things with me went crazy for a while. I got into a fight with this guy and they threw me in jail and then the guy pressed charges. I had to get a lawyer and it's all costing me a lot of money, but it should turn out all right. Then I rolled the Cadillac and broke my collar bone. I couldn't work for a couple months. I just laid there in my apartment and read books and listened to the radio. I saved the Cad's engine and some parts but all in all it's ruined. Luckily I was in the boonies and didn't get a ticket. Warren's dad came out with a flatbed and we got the Cad on it and then dropped it off at Warren's work. I picked up another Cad not too long ago and I'm going to rebuild it with the parts from the wrecked one on my days off.

I quit taking speed three weeks ago. I have a few beers but I'm off the other shit for good. It was harder than I thought, but with you leaving and then the car and the trouble with that guy, I figured it was about time.

I've decided I really am gonna be moving North. Like I always wanted. Just draw a line and go. A Northline. The farther north, the better. Away from everyone. Away from all the weirdos and freaks and Mexicans and Niggers. From everything like that. I figure the farther North you go, the better it'll be. A place saner and normal. Simpler. Maybe get a place out in the woods. Maybe Alaska. Away from Vegas anyway. I want you there with me, and I know deep down you want that, too. So give me your phone number. I'll come up in a couple weeks and we can work things out. I'm sure sorry about everything that happened, but it ain't right you just leaving either. So it makes us about even in my book so call me. I'm at the same number.

I still want you back, and will see you in a week or so.

I love you

Jimmy

She burned the letter in the sink and started crying. She couldn't stop thinking about him and her lost baby. She started to hyperventilate and her stomach got upset. She tried to lie in bed but she was too nervous. She called the phone company and changed her number in case her mother had given it to him. She knew she should move again, to a different town, but she was worn out and just the thought of it made her anxiety worsen.

After a while, just being in the apartment frightened her so she got dressed and headed downtown. She passed Louis's Basque Corner and the Last Dollar bar, St Vincent's thrift store, and the Fireside Liquor Store.

It was just past noon when she walked into Doc Holiday's. The bar was long and narrow and rundown. There was a jukebox playing. The bartender wore mirrored sunglasses and his hair was cut short, shaved on the side like a military recruit. He wore a long sleeved brown shirt, and his hands were covered in home-made tattoos. The girl sat at the bar and ordered a vodka and 7UP. She paid for it, drank it, and then four more after it. Three hours later two men, both dressed in suits, sat near her. Then they came over to her.

'My name is Red,' one of them said. He put his hand out, but she didn't take it. He was dressed in a blue suit and wore rings on each hand. His hair was red and blown dry with gel. He wore cologne and there was a gold chain hanging from his neck.

'I work down the street at City Pawn. His dad owns the place.'

'Hi,' the other man said. 'My name is Marty.' Marty had short brown hair, wore a green suit, and was built thick, stocky. He was overweight and had acne scars all over his face.

'Hello,' she said drunkenly.

Red bought them all a round. Tears welled in her eyes. They moved to a booth. She sat in the middle between them. Marty put his hand on her leg and she let him. She sat there between them and didn't care. She had nothing left.

They led her out to their car and Marty got in the driver's seat and drove them to a house in a part of town she didn't recognize. They pulled the car into the garage. They led her into the living room and Marty turned on the stereo and shut the curtains. Red led her to a couch and she sat down while he went to the kitchen for drinks. He came back carrying three bottles of beer and a fifth of Jack Daniels.

Allison took a long drink from the bottle and fumbled for a cigarette.

'I don't know what I'm doing here,' she said barely.

Red sat down next to her on the couch and lit her cigarette. 'We're having a party, that's what we're doing.'

'Yeah,' Marty added.

Red opened a beer and handed it to her. She drank from it and set it on the table.

'Are you from around here?' Marty asked.

'No.'

'You new to town?'

She nodded.

'Where from?' Red said.

'Phoenix,' she said.

'Phoenix. Jesus, what a mess,' Marty said.

She nodded.

'Why you in Reno?' Red asked.

'What?' she said.

'Why did you come with us?'

'I don't even know where I am.'

'I know why I wanted you to come along. I thought we could all fuck.'

'Jesus, Red,' Marty said and laughed.

Allison took another drink off the beer and looked around the room.

'What about you?' Red asked.

'I don't care what happens,' she said and tears fell down her face.

Red took a long drink from his beer then set it on the coffee table, moved closer to the girl, and kissed her on the neck. He put his right hand on her leg and slowly went up it. He waited for her refusal, but there was none. Marty walked over and sat on the other side of her and felt her breasts. He clumsily took off her shirt, then her bra. Red took off her shoes, pants, and underwear. They stayed there on the couch and took turns with her until Marty left.

Red then moved her into his bedroom. He got on top of her and went inside her again. He was moving back and forth when she asked him to hit her.

'What?' he asked.

She asked him again.

So he hit her. It was with reservation, he was uncertain of doing it, but he did it.

'Harder,' she said and slowly he hit her with more force. Sometimes on the arm, then he was slapping her face.

'Harder, you fucking asshole,' she cried. But then finally he couldn't.

Her eyes were closed but tears leaked out. Her face was red from the slaps, and there was a line of blood coming from her nose.

'Please,' she said and sobbed.

'What the fuck is wrong with you?' he said and got up off her. He put a sheet over her and left the room. She could hear him in the next room moving around, and then she heard the front door shut and the car in the driveway start and leave. She lay in his room and didn't move. A lamp was on, and she stared at it. She was too drunk to get up and finally she passed out.

The house was empty when she woke. She got up, found her clothes, and put them on. She left the house as quickly as she could. It was near dawn and she had missed work. She headed down the road not knowing where she was, but hoping that eventually she'd find a main street and then maybe a cab.

THE BOTTOM

When she made it home to the apartment it was past ten. She called in at work and told them she was sick, that she had the flu, that she didn't think she'd be able to come in for the rest of the week. She hung up the phone and went into the bathroom and started the tub. She shut all the curtains and found her tape player and listened to Brenda Lee while she sat in darkness in the warm water.

Hours passed and she stayed like that. She let the cold water drain and added the hot. She didn't wash herself or do anything, she just lay there and played the tape over and over. When she finally got out she put on a T-shirt and sweat pants and went to the kitchen, took a steak knife, and sat on the floor and tried to cut her wrists.

She took the knife and pressed it into her skin, but she couldn't do it. She sat for hours that way hoping for courage. She wasn't having a panic attack. It wasn't like that. Her heartbeat was slow and steady. She was calm. As she sat with the knife she saw nothing but the facts. Her past and the things she had done. They were with her, sitting next to her. They didn't haunt her right then, they were just there and they wanted her to take the knife and cut her wrists. But in the end she couldn't make the cuts. She wished for a gun but had no strength to get one. She wished for pills but didn't have any.

She lay on the floor and fell asleep and when she woke she went back to the bathtub and started the water. She didn't eat or drink.

She lay in the tub for a while and then in her bed. She didn't watch TV or try to force herself up and fight. She collapsed. The day slipped into the next. She got up from the bed and sat at the kitchen table and again tried to cut her wrists. When she knew she couldn't, she fell to the floor and laid there and cried.

Another day passed and still she had not eaten or drunk. She didn't get up off the floor. She urinated on herself but did not move. The phone rang but she did not pick it up. She just lay there and night passed and she decided she would end herself that way. She would not move, she would not eat or drink.

She fell asleep and in a dream Paul Newman grabbed her. He was dressed as a police officer. He was older, he had gray hair, and was tired and spent and worn out.

'Enough,' he cried. 'Enough.'

There were tears in his eyes.

'Don't do this to me – please,' he begged.

He held onto her and tears fell from his face.

'I can't help it,' she said barely.

'But you can.'

'It would be easier this way.'

'Not for me it wouldn't,' he told her.

'I'm just so tired.'

'I know you are. Look, it's okay to crack, but you just can't give up.'

'Will you hate me if I give up?'

'I could never hate you."

'But I make so many mistakes. All I ever do is screw up and I'm scared all the time.'

'I know you are, but I'll help you out. You just have to try first.'

'I'm sorry, but I can't. I just can't.'

Paul held onto her. He didn't know what to say. He kissed her forehead. He squeezed her as tight as he could.

'What about the kid?' he said finally. 'What if he finds out? What if he needs you some day?'

'You think he will?'

'He might. It can be a hard world.'

'He really might need me?' she asked.

'There's always a chance. You can't risk that, can you?'

'No,' she said. 'I can't.'

When she woke, she got up and went to the sink for a glass of water. She made herself eat a piece of bread, then turned on the TV and started the tub.

After her next shift back at the Cal Neva she stopped at a mini-mart and bought a TV guide. As she walked down Second Street towards the apartment she passed an old office building, and on the door was a 'Help wanted' sign.

WE NEED YOU
No experience needed. Phone sales for Curt Vacuums.
Hours 5-9 P.M. Pay $6-8 per hour.
Contact Penny Pearson between 5-9 at 784-0345

She stopped and looked through her purse, found a pen and a piece of paper, and wrote down the number. She called about the job that evening.

'Hello,' a lady answered.

'I'm calling for Penny Pearson.'

'This is.'

'I'm calling about the job.'

'I like your voice,' the woman said. 'Tell me something about yourself.'

'My name is Allison Johnson. I used to have an old Curt. It was my mom's. Our dog chewed the cord in half but my mom's old boyfriend fixed it. It was bright orange. It howled, there was something wrong with it, but it still worked good.'

'Do you need the job?'

'Yeah. It's a second job. I need to stay busy.'

'You mind people hanging up on you all the time?'

'I don't know. I've never done phone sales.'

'You mind overweight forty-three-year-old women who smoke?'

'No,' the girl said.

'Then come down tomorrow evening, say around five. You know where we're at?'

'Is it where the help wanted sign is? Is it in that building?'

'It is, hon. Number four.'

'I can be there.'

'I hope that you are,' the woman said and hung up the phone.

The next evening the woman opened the door to room number four and stood blocking the entrance with her body.

'You must be Allison,' she said and put out her hand. 'I'm Penny Pearson.'

The woman was five feet eight inches tall and weighed nearly four hundred pounds. Her hair was dark brown and pulled back in a braid that ran down to her waist. She was dressed in a faded blue jogging outfit and white socks and sandals. There was a heavy stream of sweat leaking down her brow.

'The first thing you got to realize with this sorta job is that there's no dress code. You look nice, don't get me wrong, and that's okay, but I guess what I'm saying is that you don't have to.'

'I didn't know.'

'That's why I'm telling you. Your desk is near the window. I put out a W-2 and an application for you to fill out. You can start there, and while you're busy with that, you can listen to me on the phone. It's a real battle. You got yourself into something this time,' she said, and laughed.

The room was small, barely able to fit in the two full size gray metal desks, the green metal bookcase filled with boxes, and the color TV which sat on a half-size refrigerator. The walls were white but smoke-stained, fluorescent lights hung from overhead, and posters of Curt brand vacuum cleaners took up the available wall space. The girl sat at the desk, took a pen from her purse, and filled out the forms while she listened to the woman make calls.

'Hello, hi there, I'm Penny with Curt Vacuums. Would you care to get one of your carpets professionally cleaned by a Curt Vacuum representative? It's free with absolutely no strings attached except to experience the fine quality and hardworking ability of *a genuine dry shampooing Curt vacuum*.' She paused for a second. 'Well, thank you anyway,' she said and hung up. She lit a cigarette and dialed the next number.

'Hello, hi there, I'm Penny. Would you care to get one of your carpets professionally cleaned by a Curt Vacuum representative? It's free of charge with absolutely no strings attached except to experience the fine quality and hardworking ability of *a genuine dry shampooing Curt vacuum*.'

The girl finished the forms and waited.

'Tonight, you just listen,' the woman said to her in between calls.

At three minutes to nine o'clock Penny lit a cigarette, went to the fridge, took a can of cream soda, and opened it. 'We're done for tonight. Not much of a job, but at least it's something. I signed twenty tonight, if you can get ten then you're worth keeping. It's not bad when you get used to people yelling at you, threatening your life. You have to take those things in your stride. It doesn't mean anything if you can look at it right. What do you think?'

'I don't know,' the girl said. 'I can give it a try. I'm not the strongest on the phone, but I like the hours.'

'It's not for everyone. During the day I'm a travel agent and with all the horrible things happening to us with the internet and the airlines cutting commissions I decided to get an extra job and try to save money.'

'How long have you worked here?'

'Seven years,' she said and laughed. 'Stupid, huh?'

'I don't know,' the girl said and tried to smile.

'Well, anyway, we'll get to know each other. I usually give a week to a girl so she can get the hang of it. Paid, of course. If by then you're not signing up at least ten people a night then I'll have to let you go. Don't feel bad if you don't make it.'

'Can I ask you a question?'

'Sure,' Penny said and took the sweat band from her head and set it on the table.

'Why would you give away a free shampoo and carpet cleaning?'

'It's door to door sales. We have three reps out there. I set up appointments and give the info to them, then they take over. The vacuums run up to two thousand dollars so the salesmen can really make a buck if they're good.'

'That much for a vacuum cleaner?'

'I know,' the woman said.

'Who would buy something like that?'

'Old ladies, rich people, people with no idea about money, who knows? It's the salesmen, too. They go in, some are really good, and they go around and show you how dirty and awful your place is. They vacuum your couch, curtains, a sure winner is vacuuming your mattress. All that dead skin, dust, hair, it takes it all. They show the customer each time they make a pass what exactly comes up. It's sick the things it sucks up. Sometimes those reps are in the customer's house for a couple hours.'

'I wish someone would clean my carpets, they're awful.'

'Well, if you stay on, I can borrow one of the demo models and lend it to you. They are pretty damn good. Tomorrow I'll start you calling. There's a sheet on the desk that tells you what to say. If you're good you'll ad lib the rest. Things to remember. Don't give your last name. If they ask for it, make up a false one. It's against company policy to do so, but believe me people get angry. Don't give out our address, under any circumstances. And always remain calm. If they threaten your life or say they're going to come down and kill you, you have to remember we have a blocked number. Also, flirt. If it's an old guy or any sorta guy just flirt, it's usually a quick sale. Old women – call them ma'am, be gentle. Young women – well, good luck.'

'All right,' Allison said.

'You want a cream soda?'

'No thanks,' the girl said.

'You should have one. It might be the only thing you get out of this job.'

She thanked the woman and walked over to the fridge, took a soda from it, and sat back down at her desk and opened it.

'So what's your other job?'

'I work at the Cal Neva, in the Top Deck restaurant.'

'I love their corn beef and cabbage. At least once a month I go there for that. Maybe I've seen you?'

'I work graveyard.'

'If I'm gonna go there I leave right after here. Graveyard, that's late.'

'Starts at midnight,' Allison said and stood up. 'So we're done for tonight?'

'We're done for tonight.'

'I have the job?'

'Think it over. I'll be here at five. If you're not, then I'll figure you didn't want it.'

The next morning, near the end of her shift, the man with the lazy eye sat in her section. He was dressed in his work uniform.

'Coffee?' the girl said, standing in front of him with a pot.

'Yeah,' he said and yawned.

She filled the cup. 'Do you want the usual?'

'Yeah,' he said and looked at her. 'I've never told you my name, but it's Dan.'

She laughed. 'Your name tag says it.'

'I guess it does,' he said and his face reddened. 'When I was in San Francisco I bet a horse for you and believe it or not it came in.'

'It did?' the girl said. 'Oh, you went to San Francisco? I guess I remember you saying so.'

'I bet better if I do it for other people. I don't know if I told you, but I work at the VA hospital. I won a guy there a hundred bucks.'

'Really?' the girl said.

'He's just a kid. He lost both his legs. So when I saw the horses Shorty and Annie's Arab, I bet an exacta and they both came in. I about died. He'll probably have a heart attack when I tell him. Me, personally, I lost $134. But that guy did good and you did good.'

'Oh, you should keep the money you bet for me.'

'I bet on a horse named Blue Eyes. Like your eyes. It was a favorite, but I bet him anyway. It only won five dollars so I bought you a present instead of giving you the lousy five.' He reached into a paper sack and took out a snow globe.

She looked at it. She didn't want to take a gift from him. She didn't know him and wasn't sure what he meant by giving it, but when he handed it to her she took it. The dome said 'San Francisco' on the bottom, and inside it, in the water, was the Golden Gate Bridge, and on the back a picture of the city skyline. She shook it and watched as the fake snow fell on the bridge and down on the plastic sea.

'Thank you,' she said and put it in her apron.

'It's not much,' he said.

'I'll go place your order then.' She turned away and went into the back and put the dome in her purse. She delivered three different orders before his order came up and she went back to his table.

'Do you have a hard time working all night?' he said as she set down the plate in front of him.

'I don't sleep very well, so no, I guess not.'

'Why don't you sleep?'

'I don't know, probably a lot of reasons,' she said uneasily.

'I don't mean to make you nervous,' he said.

'Everything makes me nervous,' she said.

'I'm sorry,' he said gently.

'I'm gonna pay for your breakfast. For the dome. Then we'll be even. I'll feel better about all this if you let me.'

'You never owed me anything, it was a gift,' he said.

'Still,' she said and then turned away.

HER SISTER

It was the middle of the day and she was in bed asleep when the phone rang. Her sister was crying, but the connection was full of static and the line went dead within a minute.

She laid in bed and waited for the phone to ring again, but it didn't. Eventually she called her mother, but her mother hadn't heard from Evelyn in weeks and didn't even have a number to reach her at. So she sat and waited, and while she did, her mind drifted back to Las Vegas and her sister and the high school.

She was twenty and working as a waitress at the Horseshoe when she got a call from the nurse at the high school her sister attended. Evelyn had passed out during history, fainted, for the second time in three weeks. The nurse told the girl to pick up her sister in the nurse's office as soon as she could.

When the lunch crowd finished her boss let her go and she drove to the high school in her mom's car and walked through the familiar halls in her waitress uniform.

The nurse's office was a small room in the corner of the building. As she entered, the nurse, a thin woman with blonde hair, looked up from her desk and smiled.

'You look just like her. You're Evelyn's sister, right? Allison?'

'Is she okay?'

'She's fine. I just think her blood sugar level was a little low. I gave her some juice and a couple of cookies.'

The woman stood and motioned for Allison to follow her. They walked back to a room and the nurse knocked on the door and entered.

'Evelyn? Are you up?'

'I am,' Evelyn said as she laid on a cot in the corner of the room. She smiled when she saw her sister standing behind the nurse.

'Did she come to break me out?'

'I think she did,' the nurse said.

'Are you okay?'

'I'm fine, Allie. I don't know what happened. I forgot to eat, I guess. I spent the night at Julie's and she doesn't eat breakfast. I guess we didn't eat dinner either.'

'You have to eat,' the nurse said.

'I know I should,' Evelyn said and smiled.

'We'll get something as soon as we leave,' Allison said.

Her sister sat up, put on her shoes, and stood. The nurse went back to her desk and Allison signed the release and the sisters left.

They drove to a Chinese restaurant, took the food to go, and drove to a movie theater. They put the food in Evelyn's book bag and bought tickets for a three-thirty matinee and sat in the back of the empty theater, eating, and waiting for the show to begin.

'The food's good this time. It's crazy to think that old man still works there. He's been there since we were kids.'

'He's a nice old guy.'

'I still can't believe I fainted. Now everyone's gonna think I'm a drug addict.'

'Did you really just forget to eat?'

'I swear. I love to eat. I don't care if I get fat. I just forgot.'

'I hate that school,' Allison said.

'Sorry I made you come.'

'It's better than calling mom. Plus I got off early and we get to see a movie. I never go to the movies anymore. No one I know likes them.'

'I like them,' Evelyn said.

'That's why we're here.'

'I hate school.'

'I almost puked every morning I had to go,' Allison said.

'I just stay with Julie and her friends. But the whole thing is pretty stupid.'

'Don't drop out. I should have stayed in, it was a mistake to leave. All I did was get a job. I've never traveled or done anything else. I thought I'd do more, but I haven't done anything.'

'I wish we lived someplace else. A place where we could open a store or a coffee shop.'

'I wouldn't mind working in a library or some place like that. Where every one is quiet. I could wear nice clothes, and you wouldn't have to talk to anyone. Just file and get new books and magazines and put them in order. It's always cool in the summer and warm in the winter.'

'Sounds boring to me,' Evelyn said.

'It wouldn't be. People like librarians. No one ever yells there. People are just trying to check out books. Especially if you went to a nice library, a big one.'

'I'd rather run a coffee shop,' her sister said. 'You can't play music in a library, you can hardly talk to anyone. They get pissed if you do.'

'That's what I like about it.'

'Well then, why did you quit school if you wanted to be a librarian?'

'It wasn't one thing really,' she said and thought on it. 'I guess just being around so many people my age was enough to make me want to quit. And then everyone was always talking about going to college or going to parties. I could hardly even walk down the halls in between classes. And I didn't go to the assemblies 'cause I'd get so worried that they would somehow get my name and make me get up in front of everyone. I remember at this one assembly they called six random kids to come down to the front of the gym. It was a game. They blindfolded them and then they had to try and find different things around the gym. Everyone was laughing. It was supposed to be fun. One of the kids they called was sitting right next to me. Jesus, I never went to another one after that. And then there was Spanish class where they make you talk out loud. And in English I had to get up in front of everyone and recite a passage from Shakespeare. A hundred lines. On top of that I only had a couple friends. One of them moved and the other got a boyfriend. And I was always embarrassed about the way I looked. Then after all that I started algebra and the teacher made us get up in front of everyone and do problems and that was one class where I didn't know anything. It was horrible. He would make me go over and over the mistakes I made, but I was so nervous I couldn't listen to what he was saying. So one day I just didn't get out of bed. Mom was staying with Gary then. She didn't notice for a while and by the time she did I'd made up my mind.'

It was the last evening of her first week at Curt Vacuum, and by then the girl was averaging thirteen appointments a night. At eight p.m. she hit ten while Penny had hit twenty a half hour earlier. The woman was drunk. She sat there drinking a beer and watching TV with headphones on. When the girl hung up the phone, she took them off.

'Number ten?'

'Number ten,' Allison said.

'You want a beer?'

She nodded.

'There's a six pack in the fridge.'

The girl walked to it, took a can, opened it, and sat back down at her desk.

'You've done the best of any girl I've had in almost two years. It's your voice, you have a nice one, in a good range. Non threatening. You have good grammar.'

'I didn't even graduate from high school.'

'No kidding?'

She took a drink. 'I want to get my GED.'

'You should, you seem smart. Can you read?'

'I can read,' she said.

'You have any learning disabilities?'

'Not that I know of,' she said and giggled.

'Hon, you could probably go to college.'

'I don't know about that.'

'It's easy if you want it to be. I majored in business/tourism and look at me now,' she said.

The girl took a pack of Pall Malls from her purse and lit one. 'I don't know what brand you smoke but people leave their cigarettes all the time at work. I can give you them if you want. I'm trying to quit.'

'I get Camel Lights by the carton. But you could leave a pack or two around the office just in case.' She took a cigarette from a pack on the desk and lit it. 'So why did you move to Reno?'

'I just sorta ended up here.'

'You here on your own?'

'I don't have any other family here or anything like that.'

'So why'd you come?'

'I don't know.'

'Not for the scenery or the beauty,' the woman laughed.

'A lot of reasons,' the girl said and gave a half hearted smile.

'Okay.'

'You from here?'

'God, no,' Penny said. 'I got married while I was in college in San Francisco. He was in hotel management, and after we graduated he got a job here at the Virginian. So we moved. I got a job at the travel agency. We bought a house.'

'You still married?'

'No,' she said. 'Not for years. This was fifteen years ago. This was when I was skinny. When I wasn't so big.'

'You still live in the house?'

'You sure ask a lot of questions for someone who doesn't like to answer them.'

'I'm sorry.'

'I'm just giving you a hard time.'

'I didn't mean to be rude.'

'You can ask me anything.'

'I am really sorry.'

'I told you not to be, I don't mind. Like I said, I was just giving you a hard time. Yes, to answer your question, I still live in the same house. It's over near Mayberry Elementary School. You know that area?'

'No,' she said, 'not really.'

'My ex-husband, he lives in Florida now. Works for a hotel down there. He follows the money, moves every couple years. I don't mind talking about him, but it always makes me want to eat. You ever been to the Nugget?'

'The big casino?'

'No, not that one. The one on Virginia, just down the street. The little Nugget. They have a diner in the back that has the greatest burgers, it's cheap, too. The home of the Awful Awful burger. If you're not in a hurry, I'll buy you one. I'm heading there after this.'

'All right,' the girl said.

'Then let's get rid of these,' Penny said and pointed to her beer. She finished the can in one swallow.

'You drink faster than me. That's something.'

'We all have our talents,' Penny said and smiled.

It was warm inside the Nugget casino. It was half full of old men playing slots and sitting at the bar. The two women ordered drinks then walked to the back, into the small, nearly empty lunch counter, and sat.

'I used to come here three times a week when I was married. I've always been a bit overweight, but when I got married I let it go.'

'I love to eat,' Allison said.

'God, me too,' Penny said. 'I gained a hundred and seventy pounds when I was married. Can you imagine if you married someone and that happened? He'd get really mad at me, but he wasn't skinny either, not at the beginning. He loved to eat Burger King or Kentucky Fried Chicken or Jim Boy's Tacos. He could eat that stuff every day. But then I just kept gaining more and more weight. We were married for seven years, and I gained a lot each year. Then he quit eating so much. He started running, joined a gym, and quit drinking. And that made it worse for me. I started eating even more. I guess I became more and more ashamed of myself and instead of trying to stop I kept eating. And during this whole time, of course, he starts looking better. I guess I caused that in him. It's crazy to think, but I disgusted him to the point that he decided to take care of himself. And that made it worse for us. He wouldn't sleep with me anymore, and he got less and less romantic, and he was a pretty romantic guy. It was subtle, it wasn't like anything happened overnight. It happened as slow as me gaining the weight. In the beginning we were like rabbits. Then that disappeared, but you hear about it happening like that, and you think maybe that's the way it's supposed to be. I'd justify it. And then when he finally left, I thought I'd lose the weight, that it was him, and him being so critical of me that caused me to eat so much. But then after him I still couldn't stop, and finally I just accepted myself, and that was – well, I came to that conclusion maybe a week ago,' she said and giggled.

'I'm sorry,' the girl said.

'Don't be sorry, hon,' she said. 'Men are a pain in the ass. I'd rather sit at home with the TV and a few snacks than have to watch sports and do laundry all the time.'

The girl laughed. She was getting drunk. 'Love seems nice,' she said. 'Like in the movies, like with Paul Newman.'

'There aren't many of him out there.'

'I've only had two boyfriends and they both didn't work out. So I don't know anything.'

'What are you, twenty-three?'

'Yeah.'

'You've got a lot of time. You're just beginning. You just have to be careful. If you hate yourself too much you just end up with a never ending line of assholes. Believe me, since my husband left, I've had more than a few. But they say a lot of people are pretty happy.'

'I guess so.'

'I've been to counselors and dieticians and weight trainers on and off for years.'

The counter man came and set down their meals.

'I hate doctors,' Allison said. 'I haven't seen the dentist since I was sixteen. I used to go to Planned Parenthood, but I don't ever go to a regular doctor for anything. I'm always afraid they'll commit me.'

'You really think they'd commit you?'

'They probably could.'

'You seem all right to me,' Penny said and then she started eating. She didn't talk until she was done. Then she pushed her plate away and said, 'So enough about me. Tell me about your boyfriend.'

'Which one?'

'Let's start with the first one. You said you've had two, right?'

'I've had two.'

'So then your first.'

'It's pretty boring.'

'Your life can't be any more boring than my life. If it was, you'd probably be dead. You're not dead, are you?'

'No,' the girl said and smiled a little.

'Then tell me.'

'His name was Roger. He worked at a video store my sister and I went to. The store was his mother's. She was old. I think she had him when she was in her forties, because she was really old by the time I met her. She'd had some sort of job with the city and was retired when they opened the store. I don't think it was doing very good. They didn't have a lot of movies or anything, but I'd go 'cause there was never anyone in it. You could just look around forever and no one would bother you. I hate crowded stores. Anyway, he worked there at night. He was eighteen. He'd graduated high school. I was seventeen. I was working by then. He was sorta cute, I guess. He was tall, skinny, but he had muscles even though he didn't exercise or anything. He was really into computer games. The kind you play with other people. He had friends and they'd all play these games together. They'd link up their computers and have tournaments that would last all weekend. Anyway, he started giving me my movies for free, that's how we began talking and then we started going to see movies at the theater, then I starting going over to his house. Stuff like that.'

'Was he your first?' Penny said.

'Yeah, boy,' she said, embarrassed, and looked around to see if anyone was listening. 'He was the first if you'd call it that. He was really strange. I thought it was me at the time, but now I sorta think it was him. He didn't like to kiss. I don't know why but for whatever reason he didn't. It used to make me feel really bad. I'd kissed other guys. To tell you the truth I like kissing more than anything else. But he and I would never talk about it. I never asked him why he didn't like to, I just knew he didn't. So we'd just take off our clothes. It wasn't like the movies where you take them off piece by piece, and it wasn't like we ripped them off either. We'd just be in his room and we'd take off our clothes, maybe like you would if you were changing in the morning or whatever. Not romantic or anything. His room was the entire attic of this old house. It was a cool place. He had this huge space, and there were movie posters all over the walls. Science fiction movies, action movies, animation, stuff like that. His mom and dad were so old that they didn't know anything about what we were doing. So we'd lay there naked on the bed, and it was always dark in there when we'd do it, which was good for me 'cause I hated looking at my body and the thought of anyone else looking at it. I don't think I could of handled it. Then he'd put on a rubber and lay on top of me, and he'd put his thing in for just a minute, maybe not even that, and then he'd come. It was so fast,' she said and began giggling. 'He'd let out a moan, and then he'd get up and put on a robe and go to the bathroom. He wouldn't say anything at all. And he'd be gone forever, like a half hour, maybe a whole hour, I'm not joking either, and then finally he'd come back, and I'd ask him where he'd been and he'd say, "I took a bath." I was usually dressed by that point, and then he'd get a pint of ice cream from his freezer and we'd watch a movie and then he'd take me home.'

'I used to date a guy that would come in his pants,' Penny said and lit another cigarette. 'We'd be fooling around, and we'd start taking off our clothes, and all the sudden he'd start wigging out and by the time he stopped he'd of already come in his shorts.'

'That happened, too,' the girl said. 'This one time we were laying in his room, and we were naked and I don't know why but I was so insecure about him, about everything, and for whatever reason I kissed him, which I knew he didn't really like, and then I kissed his neck, and then I started kissing his chest and his stomach, and suddenly he came. It went everywhere. He was really embarrassed. He laid there for a long time, just motionless, and I didn't know what to do. I sat up on the bed and waited. "You're really boring," he finally said and got up and put on his robe and went down to the bathroom. I got dressed and waited, but I could hear the water going for a bath and so I left. And that was it. He never called me and I never called him again. I had to start going to a different video store.'

SATURDAY

She woke up the next morning on the bathroom floor. Vomit was in her hair and on her face, and all over the toilet and the linoleum floor. She remembered getting margaritas at the Cal Neva with Penny after dinner, but nothing after that. How had she gotten home? Did she go to another bar? She stood up. Her head was pounding. She looked at her face in the mirror and saw the vomit clinging to her hair. She took shampoo from the shelf and washed her hair in the sink. She started the bath, got a 7UP from the fridge, turned on the TV, and got in the tub.

She sat in the water for nearly an hour, then dressed, ate some toast and walked down Virginia Street. The cool air and the walking settled her stomach. She stopped at Foster's Deli and ate lunch and decided she'd walk to the mall and buy a pair of running shoes. Maybe every time she wanted a drink she'd just run. She'd run all the time if she had to. Every morning or night.

The mall was crowded with kids, couples, and old people. She found the shoe store and purchased the first pair of running shoes she came across.

When she got home she put on sweat pants, a sweater, and her new running shoes, and went jogging. She was out of shape, though, and pretty soon she ended up just walking through the neighborhoods, looking at people's houses. When she got home she laid in bed and watched TV until eleven o'clock, then got up, put on her uniform, and left for work.

DAN MAHONY

At five-thirty in the morning, Dan Mahony sat in the same booth he always took at the Top Deck Restaurant, in her station. He was dressed in his work uniform, but his right eye, usually half open, was closed, the lid red and swollen.

'Morning,' she said and poured him a cup of coffee.

'Hey,' he said and smiled at her. 'You have a good weekend?'

'I worked yesterday.'

'Oh,' he said. 'What about Saturday?'

'It was okay,' she said. 'Are you going to have the usual?'

'I think I'll go poached with the eggs and bacon and sourdough toast.'

She wrote the order down and left. The next time she came back it was with his food. She set the plate down on the table. He had his face two inches away from the newspaper, trying to read it.

'Are you all right?' she said.

'I hit my head on a cabinet last night. It got part of my bad eye. Sometimes my vision goes off. It's been pretty good, but whacking my head screwed me up again. Everything's been blurry for the last day. Does it look bad?'

'It looks like it hurts,' she said

'I'm the clumsiest guy you've probably ever met,' he said and shook his head. 'Last night on the radio I heard that a guy who was staying at the Eldorado got really mad 'cause he had to wait a half hour for the valet parker to get his car. When it finally came he went straight into his trunk and pulled out a weed burner. They're like little flame throwers. It's hooked up to a propane tank and it shoots out flames for burning weeds. Anyway, I guess he chased the valet parker around the lot with it, with the flames shooting out, but the valet was too fast. Those guys can run all night long. So the guy with the flame thrower eventually gives up, runs out of energy, and then gets caught by security. I guess now he's in jail. I'm trying to see if it's in the paper but I can't focus worth a shit.'

'That's a funny image,' the girl said.

'I thought so, too,' Dan said and looked at her.

'You don't mind that I eat here every day, do you?'

'No,' she said.

'I ate here before I met you. I just like sitting in your section is all.'

'It's all right.'

'Sorry if the snow globe was too much.'

'It wasn't too much.'

'Did you like it even?'

'I put it in my kitchen, on a shelf.'

'I'm glad,' he said. 'I really am.'

WAITING OUTSIDE ON A BENCH

The next morning on her way home from work she walked down Virginia Street to the mall. It was still early out. The shops were just opening and she went into a department store and bought a pair of long underwear. As she walked out into the parking lot she could see a Babies R Us store in a strip mall across the street. She tried not to go there. She knew it was a bad idea, but couldn't help it. She made her way over and went inside. She looked up and down the aisles, staring at the different products, passing couples and mothers with kids along the way. She saw the strollers and the cribs and the toys and heard the sounds of kids talking and babies crying.

Finally she left and sat on a bench outside the building. She couldn't leave. She sat there for nearly two hours hoping that somehow her baby would pass her. She pictured the man and the woman that took him that day in the hospital. Maybe they shopped at this store. Maybe they would walk past her with her son. She just wanted to see her baby, at least for a moment, to make sure he was okay. To see what he looked like, to make sure the couple were an all right couple, that they were good parents, that they cared for him and protected him.

Penny was doing her nails. The TV was on, but with the sound off. She had a forty-two-ounce cup full of ice and vodka and orange cream soda. It was nearing eight p.m. and she had twenty-five confirmed appointments.

Allison sat at her desk, staring out the window. Below, on the street, a man was trying to push a car, an early 1980s Honda Civic, down First Street. Cars were lined up behind him unable to pass. They started honking. The man wouldn't move the car to the side of the road. He just kept going the best he could down the center of the lane.

'Look out there.'

'I bet he's a speed freak,' Penny said when she saw him. 'He's too skinny to be that strong.'

'Boy, I hate cars.'

'How many confirms do you have?' Penny asked. She pulled herself away from the window and sat on the edge of Allison's desk.

'I'm at sixteen.'

'You're seriously the best girl I've had in a long time. How about we call it a night and go to Baskin Robbins? We'll clock out that we left at nine.'

Allison kept her eyes out the window. 'All right,' she said. 'I wonder how far that guy will push the car?'

'It reminds me of the time my ex-husband and I were in the parking lot of Home Depot. This guy had a little car like the one down there. He was trying to push it, but he had three little kids in the back seat, and his wife in the front seat, in the driver's seat. It was in the summer, so it was hot out, and he was trying to push start the car. We walked over to him and asked if he needed help. It was over a hundred degrees out. Those poor kids stuck in the back, you had to feel for them. You could see them sweating. Kids don't usually sweat, but these kids were wet with it. I don't know why he didn't let them get out of the car and stand in the store, or at least in the shade. So anyway my ex-husband talks to the guy and then we start pushing, me, my ex-husband, and this guy. He was a horrible looking guy. It breaks my heart just thinking about him and his poor kids. We help push the car and we get it up to a decent speed, but the woman, his wife who was behind the wheel, didn't know how to compression start it, 'cause she kept letting the clutch out in first, and the car would just sputter and stop. We weren't going fast enough for that. We tried it once more, then my ex-husband told the guy that they should let the clutch out in second. The guy just turned to my ex-husband and told him that you had to compression start in first. You had to be there for the way this fella said it. So my ex-husband just looked at me and then back at him and told the guy good luck and we walked away. The guy stood there and screamed at his wife, and then his kids started crying.'

'Poor little kids,' Allison said, still looking out the window.

'It's Baskin Robbins time, hon. Give me your confirms and let's get the hell out of here.'

Penny drove a new silver two-door Cadillac Seville. But even with the seat all the way back her stomach touched the steering wheel and as she drove you could hear the shortness of her breath. The girl sat next to her looking at the dashboard.

'This is the nicest car I've ever been in.'

'My dad runs a Cadillac dealership in Manteca, California.'

'So you've always driven nice cars?'

'Yep,' she said.

'Boy, that's something.'

'So what's your viewpoint on marijuana?'

'I don't smoke before work or anything like that, if that's what you're asking.'

'I don't care if you do. Maybe you should.'

'I know I'm a jumpy person,' the girl said.

'You're fine. That's not why I'm asking.'

'Still, I'm sorry if I am,' she said.

'All I'm really asking is that if I smoke a joint before we eat ice cream, are you going to freak out?'

'Oh no, I don't care about that.'

'Good,' Penny said and laughed.

They parked in a strip mall that held the Baskin Robbins and took a space in the dark, away from any street lights. Penny took a joint from her purse, lit it, and put in a CD of Neil Diamond.

'Neil Diamond's a good singer,' the girl said, looking out the window.

'He's my favorite man.'

'He'd be a good husband, probably,' the girl said.

'Believe me, he would be better than that,' she said and a trail of smoke left her mouth.

'My mom listened to him all the time.'

'Every good woman should,' Penny said and coughed. 'Are you sure you don't want some?'

The girl shook her head.

'Then let's go in. I'm starving.'

The two walked into Baskin Robbins and stood under the fluorescent lights of the empty store. A teenage girl stood behind the counter, took their order, and made the sundaes. They paid and walked back to the car and ate in darkness.

'I love Baskin Robbins. I go to this one 'cause there's never a soul in there unless it's summer. In the summer I buy my ice cream at the store. Let me tell you, it's hard when you're fat and you're buying a four scoop sundae. People look at you like you just ran over their grandma.'

'I used to work there when I was in high school, but it wasn't like that one. It was busy all the time. You would have hated that one.'

'I don't think I could control myself if I worked there.'

'I used to take pints home. We had a freezer full of ice cream for a while. The lady that owned it let us each take one pint home a day. She owned it with her husband who was this really rich guy. They had investments all over, a tanning salon and a card store and two Baskin Robbins. I'm not sure what he did, but he drove a black Mercedes. Anyway, even though she had the other places she was always at the Baskin Robbins I was at. It was my first job and then she fired me.'

'I hate those rich bitches. She was probably skinny too, a blonde.'

'She was,' Allison said and laughed. 'She really was. She was dyed blonde, but I guess that qualifies as a blonde.'

'It does,' Penny said. 'This is a good sundae. That high school girl did all right.'

'She did.'

'Why'd you get fired?'

'Well, like I said it was always busy and the woman, the owner, she would get really uptight because of it. She's probably the most uptight person I've ever met. So I was always nervous and on this particular day three bad things happened. First, it was really hot out. In the summer it's always hot in Vegas, but this day was horrible. Second, it was on a Saturday so it was really crowded in the store. And the third bad thing was it was just me and her in there. Usually she just sat in the back and me and another person would work out front, but the other kid called in sick. Anyway, that day it got backed up and everybody was in a terrible mood. I thought I was doing all right, but as she would pass me, like say on her way to the register, or if she was heading to the big freezer or whatever, she'd tell me I was too slow or I was making the scoops too big or not big enough. I guess she was just sorta picking on me. I don't know why exactly. I think she hadn't worked that hard in a long time. So it goes on this way for maybe an hour or so, and then suddenly I began to hyperventilate. I was making a strawberry milkshake one moment and then suddenly I couldn't breathe. I thought I was having a heart attack. I'd never felt that way before. Everyone in the store just stared at me. Then I blacked out. The next thing I know, my mom was there with my sister Evelyn, and they took me home. I went back to work maybe a week later. The store wasn't busy at all, but the woman was there and she said a few things to me while I was making a banana split and it happened again. They had to call my mom and she had to come down a second time.'

'That must have been hard.'

'It wasn't so bad 'cause it was the year I discovered Paul Newman.'

'Yeah?'

'Well, the lady fired me after the second time so I didn't get another job or anything for the rest of the summer. I just laid around with the A/C on in the dark and rented movies. I saw Paul Newman first in *Slap Shot*, and I thought he was the funniest guy I'd ever seen. Plus he was so handsome. Then I started renting all his movies. When he's young, like in *Cool Hand Luke*, he's amazing. He's really really handsome in that. Or in *Butch Cassidy and the Sundance Kid*. But if you've ever seen *Fort Apache, the Bronx*, then you'd understand him. You ever seen that one?'

'No, I don't think so.'

'He's older in it and he falls in love with a nurse. She's really beautiful, but she's a junkie and lives in a horrible part of New York City. But she's a good person, she's just had a hard life. Paul Newman is a cop and he's tough and strong, but he's also really nice. He's just tired and worn out 'cause being a policeman in New York City is an awful job. Anyway, there's this scene where the nurse and him are together, and she's really exhausted so he makes her a bath. He puts bubbles in it and shakes the water so the bubbles get extra bubbly and he sits with her while she lays in the water. It's hard to explain, but it just kills me. As sad as it is to admit, he's probably the greatest thing that ever happened to me.'

'Paul Newman?'

'Any time I get worried or my anxieties start in, I just think about Paul Newman. Sometimes it's hard to get him here, but most

135

of the time he shows up. Ever since that summer, it's been like that.'

'You ever go see a doctor?'

'After that first one my mom thought I might have heart problems, so I went to a doctor. He took blood tests and I had a sonogram, but they couldn't find anything wrong with me. He told me to take yoga, go running, maybe see a counselor, and if that all failed, to come back. But that fall when school started it got worse again and I started missing classes and then my mom got this new boyfriend and sorta moved in with him, so I just quit going altogether. I had told myself I was gonna do something great, but then I just got a job as a waitress.'

'That's rough,' Penny said and finished the sundae. 'You still have them now?'

'You mean the panic attacks?'

'Yeah.'

'No. Not for a while, anyway.'

'Well, that's good. At least now they're over and you get to keep Paul Newman,' Penny said and put her hand on the girl's arm. 'So you'll be all right.'

'Oh, I'm fine now,' she said and tried to smile.

THE LAST DRUNK

Allison took a plastic garbage bag and put her dirty clothes in it and carried it along with a box of detergent down Fourth Street, past the rundown Morris Hotel and the boxing club, Harrison's Machine Shop, and the Rumpus Room. She came to the Last Dollar Saloon and went behind it, where there was a laundromat not much bigger than the size of a bedroom. In it were three dryers along one wall, three washers on the other, and in the middle a red picnic bench. There hung a single light bulb from the ceiling, and the place, at that time, was empty.

She looked inside two washers, made sure they were empty and clean, and put in her clothes. She took quarters from her purse and started the wash cycles, then walked into the Last Dollar Saloon with the box of detergent and sat at the bar.

It was a dilapidated old place. There was wood paneling on the walls and black and white framed pictures of Reno hung on it. There was a jukebox and tables and chairs that sat in front of two large windows that looked out onto Fourth Street. Five old men and one woman sat at the bar.

'You're back?' the bartender said when he saw her. He was an old man with a limp and a gray moustache. He had a beer in his hand and a deep, cigarette-scarred voice. 'I haven't seen you in a couple of weeks. You doing laundry again?'

'Just put two loads in,' the girl said and sat at the end of the bar away from the others.

137

'Do you want a drink?'

'Vodka and 7UP, please.'

He went to work and brought it back to her.

'You all right?' he asked. She looked rough to him. Her eyes were puffy and bloodshot. He could tell she'd been crying.

'I'm all right,' she said, so he nodded and left her alone.

He came back five times, replacing her empties, and none of the times did they speak more than what was courtesy. It was an hour later when the girl passed out, fell off the stool, and landed on the ground.

The regulars looked at her, and the old bartender came from behind the bar and tried to wake her.

'You okay?' he said and gently shook her.

'What the hell happened?' a man said.

'I don't know, but she hit the ground hard,' the old man said.

'Come on, girl, wake up,' he said again. He waited but she didn't move. He picked her up and carried her to the back room where the pool table sat and put her down on the couch. He set a bucket near her head, covered her in a blanket he took from the office, and went back to the bar.

'What are you going to do with her?' asked the woman there.

The old bartender lit a cigarette. 'I don't feel like calling the police to carry her away. That would get her in a load of shit. I'm hoping she'll just sleep it off for a while. I should have known. I shouldn't have kept serving her. I forget in a place like this.'

He checked on her every half hour as the night went along. It was almost ten o'clock when his wife came in. She had just gotten off work and as she walked to the bar the old bartender poured her a drink and put it down and the woman took a seat in front of it.

'How are things?'

'It wasn't so bad tonight,' she said and smiled. She went into her purse and took out a pack of cigarettes and a lighter and set them on the bar. 'How about you?'

'Well, it was all right, nothing more than usual, then this young girl who comes in every once in a while showed up. She does her laundry at the place next door. Now I don't know why she does it there. She must live around here. She comes in and orders drink after drink. I gotta to tell you I wasn't paying attention. I should have been but I wasn't. She ended up passing out. I didn't want to call the police. I should have, but she reminds me of Carol a little and so I just set her down on the couch and put a blanket over her. I've been looking in on her every twenty minutes or so.'

'Let me take a look,' his wife said, lighting a cigarette. She got up off the stool and walked to the back room. The girl lay there asleep. The old woman put her cigarette out on the floor and bent over and gently began to shake her. The girl finally opened her eyes and the woman helped her sit up.

'Are you all right?' the woman said gently.

'I might be,' the girl said and the woman helped her to her feet and she walked uneasily towards the bathroom. She ran the water in the faucet hoping it would deaden the sound and then she was sick. Afterwards she put water on her face and rinsed out her mouth and walked out to the room and took her purse off the couch.

'I have to get my laundry,' she said hardly and stumbled into the pool table.

The bartender walked back to the room and stood at the entry.

'I'm glad you're up. I should have stopped serving you.'

'It's my fault,' the girl said.

'I guess you ain't much of a drinker,' the bartender said.

'No,' the girl said. 'I'm not. I've about had it with it, I think.'

'It ain't much of a habit.'

'No,' the girl said. 'I puked in your bathroom, but I think I made it all in. If I didn't I can come back and clean it up when I'm all right.'

'Look, don't worry about that. Just the next time you come in with your eyes red from crying maybe I'll just give you a candy bar and a soda.'

'I'll get fat as a train if I come in here every time I cry,' the girl said and gave a half of a smile.

'Maybe that's why everyone's so fat,' the bartender said and laughed. 'Now look, I don't know how long you've lived here, but this neighborhood's not safe at night. I'll call you a cab and have it take you home.'

'I gotta get my laundry. I forgot to put it in the dryer.'

'You shouldn't worry about that tonight. In your own bed is where you should be.'

'Thanks, but I'll be okay," the girl said and then suddenly, like that, she left the bar.

She made her way down the street and to the laundromat. She moved her wet clothes into the dryers and put the quarters in and started them. She sat down on the bench and leaned against the back wall and passed out again. When she woke it was an hour later and the woman was there folding her laundry and the bartender stood next to her smoking a cigarette.

'She's awake,' the bartender said and smiled.

'What are you doing?' the girl asked worriedly and tried to stand. She was dizzy and her stomach was upset and she was tired.

'I'm folding your laundry,' the woman said. 'How are you feeling?'

'Okay, I guess.'

'You shouldn't be doing your laundry here. There are a few places up near the university that are better, that are safer.'

'And if you have to do it here, do it during the day. In the morning. Then you won't get bothered. But like my wife said, if I were you I'd just do it somewhere else.'

The woman finished folding the last pair of pants. 'Do you want us to call you a cab?'

'I'm all right, I think,' the girl said and sat back down on the bench.

'Do you want us to walk you home? Where do you live?'

'At the Emerald Arms,' the girl muttered. 'My grandfather and I live next to each other. He's a truck driver and he's probably worried sick. T.J.Watson is his name. He used to be a professional boxer. He's as big as a building.' Then she stopped talking and suddenly laid down on the bench and passed out.

'That was fast,' the woman said.

'The Emerald Arms is just up the street,' the bartender said.

'Well, what do you want to do?'

'We could try to walk her up there.'

'I guess we could try,' his wife said.

The bartender went to the girl and tried to wake her. She said a few words and then was silent. He bent down and picked her up and carried her in his arms. The girl hardly moved at all. She didn't wake. He walked out of the laundromat and his wife followed with the bag of clothes and box of detergent.

'She's like carrying a couple sacks of concrete.'

'Be careful of your back.'

'I'll try.'

'She sure reminds me of Carol.'

'That's what's got me carrying her.'

'Do you think Carol is ever like this?'

'No,' the bartender said. 'She's got Harry to look after her. Plus she doesn't like to drink.'

'I hope you're right.'

'I hope the cops won't stop us. That would be something to explain.'

'Poor girl.'

'Jesus, you wouldn't think she'd be this heavy. She looks skinny but I swear she's made of fucking rocks,' he said and he struggled with her, nearly dropping her, but he made it across the street eventually.

In the parking lot of the Emerald Arms he set her down on the pavement and they woke her again.

'Which one do you live in?' he said to her.

The girl finally sat up and apologized. She could hardly keep her eyes open, but she told them the apartment number. They helped her up to her room. She unlocked the door and the woman set the laundry and detergent inside.

'I'm sorry,' she said and tears came down her face.

'Don't be,' the woman said. 'Just be more careful. Now lock your door and drink some water.'

'And remember the next time you come into the bar, the soda's on the house. And the chips, too. But let's lay off the booze, all right? If you go on another bender I think I'll have to be put in traction.'

That night she made her shift at the Cal Neva. When it was over she decided to take a walk by the river. The morning was cold and she left the casino and went down Second Street as the sun began to come up over the mountains. As she neared the river she looked up from the sidewalk and saw Dan Mahony walking towards her. She looked back down, hoping he would pass, but he had seen her and so had come over to say hello.

He looked tired, his hair disheveled, his face puffy and pale.

'I didn't see you in the restaurant this morning,' the girl said.

'I couldn't do it today,' he said and smiled. 'I called in sick but then I couldn't sleep.'

'Is your eye still hurting?'

'No, it's pretty much better. I hear they're finally tearing down the Harold's Club and the Nevada Club buildings. I read about it yesterday. It's not going to happen for a while, but I figured I'd just take another look at them, and then maybe get a bite to eat. Where are you headed?'

'I'm just taking a walk,' she said.

'Would you want to get a cup of coffee?' he asked.

'I've been around coffee all night.'

'I'm buying. You can drink anything you want,' he said and smiled.

'Where?'

'Anywhere you say.'

'Just a cup of coffee?'

'That's it.'

'If we go back to the Cal Neva. At the lunch counter downstairs. I'll go there,' she said.

'Good,' he said.

They walked there in silence and she ordered a cup of coffee. He ordered a donut and coffee, and they sat at the counter. She knew the cook, and felt better that he was there. He was an older married man who sometimes worked in the restaurant upstairs.

'I know you don't like answering questions,' Dan said, 'but how are you doing in Reno? It sure ain't San Diego.'

'There's some good things about it here,' she said. 'I like the weather better than San Diego 'cause you have seasons. I like that you don't have to have a car. And my family all lives here now so it's not so bad. But sure, I guess I miss the beach.'

'I've never lived anywhere else. I've driven around a lot – you know, road trips and vacations and things like that – but I've never lived anywhere else.'

'I've just been here and San Diego,' she said uncertainly and stared at her coffee cup.

'You know I ain't gonna bite you,' he said.

'I'm not scared of you.'

'You'd be awful damn meek to be scared of me.'

'You can't say that,' she said and looked at him. 'I don't know you. I don't know what you're like.'

'That's why we're having coffee. I could tell you if you want.'

'You don't have to,' she said.

'I used to be a plumber. I worked for my uncle, then I got hurt and my left hand was broken. They set it with pins but I couldn't see that well, so I couldn't be a plumber anymore. I sat around for about six months then I got the job at the VA. They give me free therapy on my hand and arm.' He took his left hand and opened and closed it in front of her. 'See, it works pretty good now.'

She glanced at his scarred hand.

'Then I got addicted to bingo. For a while I could only work part time and so I began going to the Holiday Hotel for old people bingo.'

'Why would you go there?'

'Well, old people never bother you, they're generally a lot more decent to you than anyone else. Plus they're too old and tired to do much. There's never fights or anything like that. Anyway, my uncle owns this little house on Seventh Street. I stay there, I rent it from him. It's as small as an apartment, but it's got a yard, and I have a dog named Zipper. He's a beat-up looking mutt, but he's a hell of a nice dog.'

'Zipper's a funny name,' she said.

'I found him on a job site. It was out near Stead and I was working on this new housing development. There was nothing around us at all, and it was real hot out, in the dead of summer, and there he was, just a pup, wandering out in the sage brush. I have no idea how he got there. But I remember seeing something move, and for a while I thought it was a rabbit or maybe a cat, but it was too slow, you know? It was just stumbling around out there. Finally I went to take a look and there he was. His tongue hanging out, about dead. He was the skinniest little pup I'd ever seen. So that night I went over to my sister's house for dinner and I brought him with me. My niece, who's just a kid, not even in school yet, started calling him Zipper and so it just kind of stuck.'

'It's a good name.'

There was a woman who started screaming. The alarm on her slot machine rang. She'd hit a jackpot. They both looked over at her and watched.

'Do you gamble?' Dan asked her.

'No,' she said and finished her coffee.

'I just bet horses if I do anything,' he said, noticing her empty cup, and he went on talking because of it. 'I used to have this friend when I was in school, and he was a big kid. He was Italian and he was real hairy. He could grow a moustache by the age of fifteen. So he looked old. When we were in high school he'd play twenty-one at the rundown casinos that wouldn't kick him out. He'd borrow money from all his friends, take money from his folks, get money however he could so he could gamble. Sometimes he would pay me just to stand behind him. He didn't like going alone. But afterwards, if he'd won, he'd buy me dinner at a steak house and maybe give me twenty bucks.'

'I've never heard of a kid like that. What's he do now?'

'He works at a wrecking yard,' he said and laughed.

The cook came by with a pot of coffee to fill both their cups. Dan glanced at her to see if she was going to take another, and when she did, he relaxed.

'You from a big family?'

'I guess,' she said and put sugar in her coffee. She stirred it with a plastic fork.

'I have a sister in Fallon. She married a guy in the military out there. He's a pretty all right guy even so. I mean, he treats her nice and everything. I don't see them much even though they're only an hour away. They have a couple kids. She's older, she's ten years older than me.'

'I have a brother and a sister,' the girl said. 'My brother's a police officer. He lives just up the street from me with his family. My sister's in Mexico with her boyfriend. I don't know anything about Mexico. She hardly ever calls, and when she does it's only for a couple of minutes. I hope she's all right down there.'

'Where in Mexico?'

'Down near Puerto Vallerata.'

'I think that's a real tourist sort of place. You ever been out of the country?'

'No,' she said and shook her head. 'I've been around Southern California and Arizona and that's about it. My dad takes us to the Grand Canyon every year. He grew up on a ranch near Flagstaff and every summer we have a huge family reunion. My sister and I, we always lived together, and now I just have roommates. I've never been away from her this long. She always makes everyone feel optimistic about things.'

'How about you?'

'Me?'

'Are you an optimist?'

'I try,' she said, 'but I'm not like her.' She paused and took a drink of coffee, then put the cup down and stared into it. 'To be honest I'm probably the opposite. I have the worst thoughts. I really do. I always think I'm gonna get run over by a bus or get murdered. That I'll get a terrible disease or go to jail forever. And the crazy thing is when I think those thoughts, sometimes it makes me happy. I don't know if happy is the right word. Maybe relieved.

I don't know, but she doesn't have thoughts like that.'

'I get thoughts like that. Everyone does, I think. Maybe it takes the pressure off. If something like that happened, then you'd be done. You wouldn't have to try anymore.'

'Maybe,' she said and suddenly stood up. 'I never thought of it like that. But I'm talking too much.'

'I don't know if you ever could,' he said and finished his coffee.

After a while she put on her coat. 'I'm sorry but I don't want a boyfriend,' she said to him.

'Me neither,' he said and smiled. He stood up. 'I just think we should go play bingo some time. At the Holiday. During the day. We could meet there. You could bring your roommates, or bring your family.'

'I'm sorry,' she said, 'but I don't think so.'

'All right then,' Dan said. 'That's okay, too. At least we had this cup of coffee.' He put on his coat, said goodbye, and walked away. She watched him as he wandered through the rows of slot machines, then sat back down and ordered breakfast.

THE GIRL IN THE CHECKOUT LINE

There was a young woman with a child standing in line in front of her at the grocery store. Allison had just gotten off shift and was dressed in her work uniform. It was eight in the morning, there was only one clerk working and she was buying bacon, ice cream, the *National Enquirer*, and three glazed donuts. The woman in front of her had a baby boy in her arms. He was playing with her hair. The line was long and slow. The woman had diapers, frozen dinners, milk, jars of baby food, and boxes of cereal in the cart. She was young, she didn't even look twenty. She had brown hair down to her shoulders and was dressed in jeans and a sweater.

The boy took a barrette from his mother's hair. He held it in his hand then threw it to the ground in front of Allison. The young woman turned around.

'I'm sorry, did that hit you?'

'Oh no,' Allison said and bent down and picked up the barrette and handed it back to her. 'He's got a good arm, though. Maybe he'll be a baseball player. How old is he?'

'Two,' the woman said

'Is he yours?'

'Yeah,' she said and rolled her eyes. 'All mine.'

'He looks like you.'

'Yeah, he does, doesn't he? Isn't this line taking forever? I have to take the groceries by my place, then drop him off at my mom's, then I got to go to work, all in an hour. My husband's out of town for two weeks and it's driving me mad.'

'Good luck,' Allison said and smiled.

'Thank you,' the woman said and turned around and the line slowly crawled forward.

In the parking lot she watched the woman load her groceries into the bed of an old pick-up truck and then put her son in the cab, in a car seat, and drive off. As she walked down Wells Avenue towards her apartment she began to cry. She sat down at a bus stop bench at some point and it wasn't until later, when she arrived home, that she realized she had left her groceries there, on a bench more than a mile away.

She sat at her kitchen table and took the only beer from her fridge and opened it. She took the notebook from her purse, opened it to an empty page, and started writing.

What kind of person does what I did? That girl, I wish I was that girl. I wish I was her. She didn't give up. She didn't fuck up her life like I did. I wish I could just disappear. I wonder every day where he is, I wonder what he's doing. Every time I look at my body I see him. Every time I take my clothes off I see him.

She paused and drank from the can of beer. Her anxiety welled and again she began to cry. She stood, then walked to the kitchen. She took a worn out steak knife from a drawer, and stood over the sink and pressed the knife into her wrist. Blood slowly began dripping into the steel sink. She stood there trying to push it in harder, but there was too much pain and she couldn't. She sat down on the kitchen floor, crying, and held a dish towel on her bleeding arm.

DESSERT

It was past nine and the two women left the Curt Vacuum office and walked towards the Eldorado Casino and its dessert buffet. It was a cold evening with a storm threatening. They were both smoking cigarettes and wearing winter coats and hats. The streets were nearly empty and they walked in silence.

Penny led her through the casino, past the tables, the endless rows of slot machines, the bars, up to the second floor and the dessert buffet. She ordered a slice of chocolate cake, an éclair, a dish of soft serve vanilla ice cream, and three chocolate chip cookies. The girl stood behind her and ordered a cup of coffee and two éclairs. They sat in a booth and ate and watched the gamblers pass in front of them.

'Hon, you got to try this cake,' Penny said and cut a piece with her fork and set it on a napkin in front of the girl. 'You do like chocolate cake, don't you?'

'Everyone likes chocolate cake,' she said and put the cake in her mouth.

'It's good, isn't it?'

'Next time I'll get that.'

'It's one of their mainstays. They have it here all the time,' Penny said and noticed the white bandage wrapped around the girl's wrist.

'Have you had that bandage on all night?'

'Yeah,' Allison said.

'What happened?'

'I was busing a table 'cause we were short a busboy and I cut myself on a knife.'

'Must have been one mean knife,' she said and looked at the girl in the eyes. 'Does it hurt?'

'No, not really.'

'Good,' Penny said and put her fork down. 'I'm eating too fast.' She took a drink of water and lit a cigarette, 'Hon, I don't mean to pry, but how's your love life?'

'My love life?'

'Yeah,' she said. 'I mean after that video clerk. You had another boyfriend, didn't you?'

'Yeah, I did but I don't have a love life now.'

'I haven't had anything in three years. You just split up with number two, is that right?'

'A while ago.'

'Was he a good one or a bad one?'

'A bad one.'

'I don't want to pry, but still.'

'I guess he had some good points. He was strong, he was pretty good looking, too. He made me feel safe a lot of the time. I guess I needed that. At the beginning I did. That was something he had. But he was an asshole. He could be really mean.'

'How mean?'

'I don't know,' Allison said. 'He used to get in fights all the time.'

'He ever hit you?'

'Yeah,' she said and her voice got quiet. She quit looking at Penny.

'My guess was something like that.'

'Why would you say that?'

'You just got that skittish way about you.'

'He used to get mad 'cause I'd get too drunk and embarrass him. But he liked to drink all the time, and he wanted me with him. We were always going out. I'm not very good at being around a lot of people. It makes me nervous and then I start drinking to calm down, and before you know it I'm in trouble. The problem with him was I never knew what would make him happy or pissed off. Something that had always made him happy all the sudden would make him mad. You never knew. Sometimes he'd get so mad and there was nothing I could remember doing wrong. Then a bunch of horrible things happened and so I left.'

'Left Las Vegas?'

'Yeah,' she said and took a drink of coffee. 'You're not going to tell anyone anything we're talking about, are you?'

'No, hon, I don't operate that way.'

'I would never tell anyone anything we talked about. Usually the only person I talk to is my sister, but she's gone and I don't know how to get hold of her.'

'She's in Mexico, right?'

'Right,' Allison said.

'Does your boyfriend know you're here?'

'He found out,' the girl said. 'He gave a letter to my mom and she sent it to me and it said he was coming to find me here.'

'You think he will?'

'He might, I don't know,' she said. 'Now every time I see a guy that sorta looks like him, I get nervous.'

'That's a hard way to live. You should contact the police. Get a restraining order against him. At least call them and tell them your situation.'

'I know,' she said and looked down at her plate.

'You know what you got to do,' Penny said and put out her cigarette. 'You gotta do something nice for yourself. Get your GED. That would be a step. It would give you confidence. In the meantime get your hair done. You could be a pretty girl if you got that hair out of your face. I know a woman, I'll give you her name.'

'I'm gonna sign up for a class to get my GED.'

'I could loan you the money.'

'I couldn't take your money. I have enough in savings.'

'Then will you at least get your hair cut on me? Sometimes you gotta eat and sometimes you got to buy clothes and sometimes you got to get your hair done. That's the only sound advice I can give you tonight.'

'Okay,' the girl said.

'You promise?'

'I promise,' she said.

THE NIGHTMARES

It was weeks later that she had the nightmares about the baby, about Jimmy, about what had happened that night with the Mexicans. They were strange and they twisted the facts and the outcome. They appeared out of nowhere, like blood leaking from a nose. She didn't know what to do about it. For a while they came every time she slept. She tried to change the food she ate, she tried to sleep with the heat off, with the TV on. She tried everything she could think of.

Sometimes she'd lay there in a cold sweat, panicking, awakened suddenly from a nightmare. Then as if it played before her on a screen, she'd remember her past and what she had done and what she had seen and who she was.

The tattoos, the swastika, the WCOTC emblem were inked when she was half passed out in the bedroom of a tract house. Jimmy and his friends Warren, Lou, and Harlan lived together twenty miles east of Las Vegas on four acres.

They'd have parties there. Bands would play. Lou and Harlan were followers of the white supremacist group World Church of the Creator before it fell apart. They'd hand out pamphlets and have kegs. She'd known Jimmy for six months. Lou was a tattoo artist and one evening he gave each of the four's girlfriends a tattoo on the small of her back. She remembered she was drunk, laying on her stomach with her shirt pushed up and her pants pulled part way down while Lou worked and Nan and Jimmy watched and drank beer. She wasn't even sure what a swastika really meant, and all she knew of the World Church of The Creator was that Jimmy liked them and they were against immigration, they were against Mexicans.

Hours later she lay in the darkness of Jimmy's room. He was quiet, whispering in her ear. In the background was the party. A band was playing in the carport and people were talking and yelling, but to her it was a thousand miles away. They lay on a mattress on the ground in the dark. There were no sheets, just an old sleeping bag and a pillow. He had lit a candle and put it at the head of the bed.

'I love you,' he told her. He was drunk and holding her. He was dressed in black jeans and a white tank top. She lay naked next to him.

He kissed her ear. 'These guys can be a bunch of morons. Eventually I'll move out on my own. We can live together and get married.'

'Get married?' she said.

'We'll save up some money and we'll leave town. We'll get a ranch up in Wyoming. I'll take care of everything. We'll have a bunch of kids and nothing will bother us.'

'I've never been on a ranch,' she said.

'Me neither,' he told her. He sat up and took a drink off a pint of Jim Beam he had next to the bed. 'But we can learn. We can do anything if we try hard enough.'

'I know we could,' she said and he laid back down next to her.

'No one will fuck with you,' he said.

'I'm not scared if you're around,' she said.

'We'll have a bunch of land and a garden. We'll have horses and dogs.'

'Can we have a hot tub?' she asked.

'We'll have a hot tub and we'll buy land near a river and in the summer we'll go skinny dipping. We'll sleep under the stars. None of this bullshit will be there. None of it.'

'What else?' she said and pulled off his shirt and began kissing his stomach.

'We'll have a room for movies. A big TV. It'll be huge and we'll have all the movies you want. All kinds. You can watch movies, anything, anytime you want.'

She sat up and took off his shoes then his pants and underwear. She felt his body. His white skin that held no tattoos.

'I'll take care of you,' she said to him and sat on top of him. 'You know I'll take care of you.'

'I know you will,' he said.

VERN'S TATTOO PARLOR

The next morning she got out of bed and looked through the phone book for a tattoo parlor. She found a place named Vern's and called and set an appointment for her day off. When the day came she went to the bank, took two hundred dollars from her account, and walked down Wells Avenue to the address she had written down. The parlor was in a small brick house, and was run by a fifty-year-old man, Vern. Tattoos covered both of his arms like sleeves. His gray hair was greased and he wore thick black-framed glasses. She went to his back room and pulled up her shirt and told him she wanted them covered. They talked of the different things he could do, and decided to make them into black stars. She laid on her stomach and he did the work in silence while they listened to talk radio.

BINGO

The restaurant was nearly empty and Dan Mahony was her only table. The girl stood in the back, and watched him from a distance. There was the scar across his face and the eye that didn't work and barely opened. His crippled hand. The way he always ate alone and was always trying to talk to her. She took the coffee pot and went to his table.

'How are you doing this morning?' she said.

'Good,' he said and smiled.

'How's your dog?'

'Same, but he licks a lot. He woke me up last night licking my arm like it was a popsicle.'

The girl laughed.

'I'll just take the regular. Let's say over medium on the eggs, bacon and sourdough toast.'

'All right,' she said and wrote down the order. She paused, then looked at him. 'I decided I think I'll play bingo with you if the offer still stands.'

'Good.'

'Good.'

'We could just meet there some time,' he said.

'I can go Saturday,' she said.

'I can go Saturday. It's at the Holiday. Do you know where that is?'

'Yeah,' she said.

'On Saturday they start at one. We could meet there at one. Outside the Bingo parlor.'

'I might bring my brother if that's okay,' she said.

'I like brothers, bring your father too.'

'My father wouldn't like bingo at all. He's a football coach. He doesn't like anything that's not related to sports.'

'Who does he coach for?'

'The university here,' she said. 'My brother's a cop, but usually he gets Saturdays off. I'll ask him if he wants to go. We usually go see a movie on Saturday, but maybe this weekend he'll want to do something different.'

'Good.'

'Well, I'll go place your order then.'

'Okay,' he said and then watched her as she disappeared into the back.

It was snowing on Saturday. She'd never been in a snowstorm and she was happy as she walked towards the Holiday Hotel. The streets were empty and the snow fell heavily and wet and stuck to the sidewalks.

Dan Mahony was waiting outside the bingo parlor when she arrived. They said hello he and led her in. They sat at the end of a long row of tables. Across from them sat a group of old women whom he introduced her to. She shook each of their hands and said hello, then took her coat off and sat down across from him.

'I'll go get us a couple games and some markers,' he said and walked to the counter. When he returned the game had begun and they listened as numbers came up. He won the fourth game and when he yelled bingo the ladies at the other table shook their heads.

'Lucky Dan strikes again,' one of the women said.

Dan stood and smiled and walked to the front and got his money, then sat down and started another game. They played four more in silence before their sheets were filled.

'Do you want to watch the snow fall? They have a diner here. We can get something to eat or a cup of coffee. There are booths that sit right next to the window.'

'All right,' she said.

He led the girl through the casino and into the diner. They sat near the window in a small booth. The snow was still falling heavy and wind gusts were making it blizzard.

'You drive down here?'

'No,' she said.

'That's a good thing with this weather.'

A waitress came and set down two menus and poured them coffee.

'Did you have a good time?'

'You mean playing bingo?'

'Yeah,' Dan said and took a sip of coffee.

'It's funny with all the old ladies. They all know you.'

'I went there a lot for a while. The old ladies, they treat you pretty good. They bake you cookies, things like that. For a long time it was the only thing that got me out of the house.'

She put sugar in her coffee and stirred it with a spoon.

'What did happen to you?' she asked.

'Well,' he said after a time, 'I was walking home through the college grounds up at UNR. It was nighttime. I was walking home from a party my cousin had. I had longer hair then, maybe it was almost as long as yours. But otherwise, I was dressed normal.

Jeans and a flannel coat, I don't know. It was late, maybe three in the morning, and there was no one around. And then four guys came up. I didn't know them. I had never seen them before. They were drunk. It seemed like they came out of the air. They started saying things to me. They called me a queer. They kept yelling that at me, and then they surrounded me. I hadn't said a word and then I just started running. I didn't know what else to do. There was something going on I didn't understand. The guys were young. I don't know if they were in a fraternity or what. I didn't know what was going to happen. They chased after me. One of them tripped me and I fell, and then they just started kicking me. One of the guys bent down and started hitting me in the face. Then another one did and then another. They had to rebuild my cheekbone. They broke my arm and hand. They broke two ribs, and punctured one of my lungs. I got a concussion and my other hand was completely ruined. One of them stomped on it with his boot a few times. And then they ran off. I don't know why they did it. I laid there and I was sure I was going to die. I just laid there on the sidewalk. There was nothing I could do. I couldn't get up. Then this couple, a guy and a girl, walked by and saw me.'

'Jesus,' the girl said.

'I was in the hospital for nearly two weeks. I was stuck at home for over six. I had three different surgeries after I left. One on my face and two on my hand. I couldn't work afterwards. My hand was in a cast, and the bones were pinned with metal and screws. My bad eye couldn't focus and my good eye wasn't that great for a couple of months. I think I told you I used to be a plumber, and I liked it all right. I got to work with my uncle who's about as nice a person you'd ever meet. I was going to be part owner. But after I got out of the hospital and my mom went back to Denver, I don't know, it was hard to get out the door. I couldn't go back.'

'It's hard to leave the house when things like that happen to a person,' the girl said.

'But I went half crazy at home by myself, so I got a job at the VA. I answered an ad in the paper. I didn't even know where it was. I just figured no one else I knew would either. I've been there for almost a year now. I'm a fucking janitor. I don't do anything really. I make no real money. My hand's better and I could go back to being a plumber and making good money and being with my uncle, but I just can't. I can't barely even go to a bar where there's people my age.'

'Did they ever find who did it?'

'I couldn't really remember a face. I tried. My uncle and I used to sit outside the college in the main courtyard and watch for them as the students passed in between classes. But I couldn't remember anything.'

'I'd feel like being around old people too,' the girl said.

'I feel liked I'm marked, you know? It's not just my face and my eye. It's not just that I don't look good anymore.'

'I feel like I'm marked,' she said to him.

'I hope we're both not,' he said and tried to smile.

'Me too,' she said. 'Me too.'

'You know what's crazy is that now when I go to the hospital, with all the bad situations there, I feel more normal. It feels right. There are new guys in there from Iraq and there are guys that haven't left in years. Old vets. One guy hardly has any face. It took me six months before I could go into his room without getting sick to my stomach. It took me that long just to look at him when

I was talking to him. And I saw him every day. Every day I had to go into his room. He's a nice guy who got his face blown off when he was just done being a kid. He always makes fun of my scar and my eye. It's pretty funny if you look at it in the right light. There's all sorts of guys like that. A guy there who only has one arm, no legs. No one visits him. No one at all. He leaves for months at a time but he always comes back drunk and barely half alive. One of the doctors, the one I know, he's an alcoholic. Some days he looks so rough and raw that you think at any moment he'll just die. He gets like that, almost crazy, but I understand him, you know? I like him, I feel more comfortable around him than any of my old friends. More than my uncle even. And I never felt that way before it happened. I never would have gotten the job at the VA or any of it. I wouldn't be playing bingo with a bunch of blue-hair old ladies. Not that I don't like it – I mean, I do, I'm just different now. I mean, the only reason I eat at the Cal Neva every morning is 'cause the doctor, the one I just mentioned, said he thought I should keep trying to move back into the world. He told me I had to eat out one meal a day and it couldn't be take out. I promised him. I promised him I'd go in public at least for that. So I eat out so I can try to fit in, you know?'

'Yeah,' she said.

'Stupid, huh?'

'I don't have a brother who's a cop,' the girl said.

'You don't?' he said and laughed.

'No,' she said.

'Your dad a football coach up at the university?'

'No,' she said and took a drink of coffee. 'I don't know where he is. I haven't seen him in years, not since I was a little kid. He cheated on my mom with a cocktail waitress and left town with her. The last we heard he was in Atlantic City working at a casino there.'

THE HOUSE

She was standing outside on Virginia Street and it was just past dawn and she had gotten off work early. There was ice on the street and the blue glow of the casino lights shone down upon it. It was quiet. Then suddenly there were the sounds of sirens. She looked down the street and saw two fire trucks come towards her. Their sirens were blaring, their lights flashed, and she watched them as they rushed by her. She looked past them to see where they were going. She looked for smoke or fire but she could see none.

She began walking home, and it was then that the thought of the burning house came to her. The time when Warren, JT, Jimmy, and she were in the car. Jimmy and she in the back. They were drinking from a bottle of Jim Beam, chasing it with Coke, in the darkness of a parking lot.

'When I was a kid,' Jimmy said, 'this neighborhood was safe. It was a good place to live. No one fucked with you. Your sister could walk down to the store in the middle of the night. My mom would send me to the store for stuff when I wasn't even eight. Now she won't even go there herself. Now a guy that doesn't even speak English owns it. Allison's neighborhood's the same. Now there's fucking cars on the lawns, gunfire at night. I'd move like every other white motherfucker, but everything in this goddamn city is too expensive. We can't all move, and why should we? Anyway, how many fucking times does a person have to move? I mean, are we gonna have to go to one of those gated communities like all the other pussies who are scared? This is my fucking neighborhood and I'm not gonna keep giving it to some wetback motherfucker who comes here illegally. We spend a fucking fortune taking care of illegals. We give them better medical care than we even give our own. And now they want everything to be bilingual. The fucking Italians, the Germans, the Polish, the Chinese, they all learned the language, didn't they? They had respect for the country, for what the country meant. They embraced it, not took from it, not stole from it. It's up to us to stop it. No one else is gonna do it. The politicians don't give a shit 'cause they're getting their fucking houses cleaned and their lawns done by a bunch of illegal border jumpers. I mean, don't get me wrong, I understand why these fuckers come over. I mean, they've fucked up their country, they've ruined their homeland, so they come over here and now they're doing the same. It's time to stop it and the only way I can think of to do it is one neighborhood at a time.

'That's why I wanted us here tonight. I saw them over there with a real estate agent, and I called the agency and the wetback motherfuckers closed on the house today. No one lives in it right now. That's the thing. It's vacant, so we're not going to hurt anyone. But it's a block from my folks' house and soon an army of wetbacks will be in there and I'm tired of it. There's an alley behind the house. I got four two-gallon plastic gas jugs in the trunk. We park the car behind the 7-11 down the street. There's no houses there around it, just the vacant lot. We'll cover the plates on the car, and then we'll walk down the alley until we get to the house, and then we'll go in the backyard. Make sure you stay in the back otherwise people could see. And no talking. No matter what, no talking.

Then leave the gas jugs with me. I'll burn them. I'll stay after you all leave and light it. We'll meet back at the car and no running. Just walk back. I'll be five minutes behind you. If something goes wrong, it's each man for himself, and we'll meet when we can. Just go by foot, hide in a yard, whatever it takes. But if we're going to do it, I need to know now if everybody's in. 'cause I won't do it unless we all do it.'

'I'm in,' Warren said. 'I agree with Jimmy. We got to start neighborhood by neighborhood, and we might as well start now.'

'I'm in,' JT said and looked at Jimmy.

Jimmy looked at Allison in the dim light.

'How about you?'

They walked down the alley in silence. The night was clear and there were stars overhead. Dogs barked in the distance, but none in the immediate neighborhood made a sound. They came to the house and went through the gate and through the yard to the back porch. Each of them began pouring the gasoline. JT found an unlocked window and poured gasoline inside the empty kitchen. Allison poured her jug against the back door and all along the wood siding. When her can was empty she went to Jimmy and gave it to him. The others did the same and then quietly walked towards the street.

Jimmy kneeled down by the porch of the house and looked at his watch until five minutes had passed, then he took the last of the gas and soaked the three plastic jugs with it, placed his jug with them and lit them. With another match he then lit the walls of the house and threw another through the open window. He turned around only once as he walked down the alley. He could see the flames growing and the smoke appearing. The red and gold and the black smoke together. The fire had caught and he knew then the house would be ruined. He knew the family who'd bought the house would be called in the middle of the night or in the morning and told the news.

Hours later he and Allison were at a party in the desert. They walked alone and sat in the dirt among the sage brush.

'I counted on you and you came through for me,' he said to her.

PHASES AND STAGES

Dan Mahony didn't come into the Top Deck restaurant for two weeks. He had given the girl his address and his phone number on the back of a napkin some weeks earlier, though, and so one afternoon the girl walked to his house.

She went to Seventh Street and took his address from her pocket and began reading the numbers on the homes until she came to his. It was a small house set back from the road and surrounded by a yard. The grass was brown and half covered in leaves. There was an old cottonwood tree in the center of the lawn, its branches almost reaching from one side of the yard to the other. There were a few pine trees scattered along the chain link fence which surrounded the property.

The house itself was brown and had a red door. There was an aluminum boat to the right of it, set on a trailer, and an old Honda dirt bike locked to a fence post.

As she came to the metal gate and opened it, a dog appeared from behind the house and slowly walked towards her wagging his tail. The girl bent down and petted him.

'Hello, boy,' she said softly.

She walked to the front door and knocked, but there was no answer. The curtains were closed and she couldn't hear anything inside. She knocked once again and was just beginning to turn away when the door opened.

Dan Mahony stood in front of her. He was wearing a pair of

faded jeans with holes in the knees. He wasn't wearing a shirt and his hair was in disarray. He hadn't shaven in weeks and looked as though he'd just woken up.

'I tried to call, but no one ever answered,' she said and smiled. The dog was at her feet and she bent down and pet him again. 'I like your dog.'

'He's a good one,' Dan said and rubbed his face to wake up. 'Let me put on a shirt. Come on in.'

The house inside wasn't much, just a main room, a bedroom, a kitchen, and bathroom. The main room had a wood stove, and it was burning, and the inside was warm. There was an old couch covered by a dark blue sheet against the wall, and a TV set on a plastic milk crate in front of a window. Next to it was a stereo set on an old wooden crate with stacks of CDs next to it. The walls were white and were bare except for a large black velvet painting of a Mexican bandit smoking a cigarette. His scarred face, his faded sombrero, his leather ammunition belt across his chest, his eyes staring off into the distance.

The room was cluttered and un-kept, clothes lay on the floor, newspapers and fast food bags were scattered everywhere. The floors were carpeted in worn out brown shag. There were holes in it where traffic had been the highest, with duct tape surrounding the holes to hold the carpet down. She took off her coat, gloves, and hat and set them on the couch and stood next to the stove to warm herself.

Dan reappeared from his bedroom wearing a red flannel shirt. His hair was wet and combed and he wore brown work boots.

'I'm glad you came,' he said and smiled.

'This is a great place,' she said. 'I like the wood stove. I've never lived anywhere that had a fireplace. I'm sorry to bother you, but I hadn't seen you in the restaurant for a long time. I was wondering if everything was okay.'

'Well,' he said and opened the curtains, letting light in the front room. 'I guess I just hit one of those phases, you know?'

'What kind of phase?'

'The sorta phase where you can't get out of bed,' he said and smiled again. He leaned against the wall and looked at her. 'You want something to eat, to drink?'

'All right,' she said. 'I'll have something to drink if you have it.'

'Come into the kitchen,' he said.

She put her hands close to the wood stove and rubbed them, then followed him into the kitchen. It was small like the rest of the house, and the paint was old and faded and lime green in color. There was a sink and some wooden shelves along the walls, an old refrigerator, a gas stove, and a table and two chairs set by a window. A calendar hung near a clock on the only bare wall. The calendar was large and had a photo of a woman in a bikini. Underneath it read 'Johnson Plumbing Supply'.

There were dishes stacked high in the sink and the small table was covered in fast food bags, unopened mail, and soda cans. The room smelled of garbage and rotting food.

'Sorry about the mess,' he said and sat at the table. 'You can get anything in the fridge. I could make us some coffee, too.'

'I think coffee would be good for both of us. But I can make it, you just tell me where everything is.'

'All right,' he said. He opened the curtain covering the kitchen window and sat back down. Outside, behind the house, was an alley, and before it a concrete car port where his black Ford pickup sat.

The girl made the coffee, then washed two mugs and poured them each a cup. She found a container of sugar and washed a spoon. She looked in the fridge for milk, and a quart sat full, unopened, but expired. She brought the coffee to him and sat at the table.

'I apologize for how dirty it is in here,' he said and drank from his cup. 'It ain't always like this.'

'It's all right,' she said. 'What happened?'

'I'm embarrassed to even tell you.'

'You shouldn't be embarrassed around me. Everything makes me depressed.'

'Well,' he said, then paused for a time. 'I was waiting in line at this liquor store down the street. I was just buying a beer after work. It's on the route I walk. There were a couple guys behind me. They were young, just idiots. Maybe they were in college, I don't know. Just average looking guys, I suppose, but more than anything I guess they seemed a lot like the guys who beat me up. They made me nervous at any rate, and I had a handful of change I was gonna use to buy the beer, and I got so nervous I dropped the change on the floor, and it ran all over. I got on my knees trying to grab it all and when I looked at them, really just glanced at them, they were staring at me. I guess 'cause I was so clumsy or maybe it was my eye. Anyway, then they said a couple things.' He paused again and took another drink of coffee.

'What sorta stuff did they say?'

'Ah, it was nothing really. They were idiots, you know? They were just making fun of me for spilling my change. But still, when I turned around to say something, stand up for myself, my heart just sorta fell, and when I looked at them, really looked at them, I got scared. More scared than I had been in a long time. Scared that they'd want to fight, that I'd go out into the parking lot and maybe this time I would die. Maybe they would kill me. It doesn't sound like much to get me so upset, but it did. So I just walked out of there, left my money on the floor, left the beer on the counter. What's weird is, even the guys at work, some of them are really all right, they wouldn't hurt a fly, but when they raise their voice to me, my heart just sorta sinks, I break out in a sweat. I've always been that way a little, but not like now. Never like now. That day at the liquor store nothing really happened but still I was wrecked 'cause of it. And all the way home I was waiting for them to chase me, to get me. For what? Why would they do it? There was no reason for it. But I couldn't stop that feeling. I kept turning around. I even walked down different streets and I took an alley when really I don't walk home that way. It was a horrible feeling. When I got back here I just sat in my place and I knew I was beat. So then when I woke up that next morning, I just couldn't make a go of it. Hell, it's stupid but that was a couple weeks ago.'

'I'm sorry,' Allison said and looked at him. He was staring at the ground, his two hands holding the coffee cup. 'Those guys, those guys that hurt you, they're just horrible people. That's all they are, Dan. Not everyone's like that, even though it seems like they are sometimes.'

Tears began falling from his face. 'I don't know what's wrong with me.'

She got up and kneeled in front of him. 'There's nothing wrong with you. You look different, but you're not ugly. I don't think so. Your scar makes you look handsome and your eye, it makes you look sorta tough. And think about those poor guys you were telling me about at the VA. They'd probably love to be in your shoes. To look like you, and live here, and have a dog named Zipper.'

He wiped the tears from his eyes and looked at her. 'I know,' he said quietly. 'I know all that.'

'Why don't you go take a shower and change your clothes? You should shave, too. You look better without a beard and you smell worse than your dog.'

He laughed at that. 'I probably do.'

'I'll wait,' she said.

As he walked down the short hall and into the bathroom, she found a package of garbage bags, and started cleaning the kitchen. She threw away the old food in the fridge, the empty soda cans, and all the fast food bags laying about. She opened the back door and took out two full bags of trash. She set them by the garbage can and went back in and into the living room and turned on the stereo. With another trash bag she cleaned the living room and hallway. She placed the last garbage bag out by the others, then did the dishes, and cleaned the counters.

When Dan reappeared he was clean shaven. He was dressed in black pants and a white long-sleeve shirt. He sat at the kitchen table and put on his boots.

'You look a whole lot better,' she said as she finished wiping down the counters. She stood leaning against the sink with her arms folded. Her black hair was pulled back in a pony tail and sweat gathered on her brow.

'You didn't have to clean like that,' he said.

'Sometimes having a clean place can make you feel better.'

'I kind of let things go, I guess,' he said.

'I've let a lot of things go,' she said. 'Sometime you can't help it.

Did you lose your job?'

'No,' he said and finished lacing his boots. 'The doctor I told you about, I called him and told him what happened, and anyway he understood, I guess, 'cause he told everybody I had pneumonia and I'd be out a couple weeks. Problem is, the couple weeks are about up, and I gotta go back.'

'You just got to go there then. Just show up and the rest will take care of itself.'

'I'll go, I will,' he said and smiled. 'The place sure looks nice.'

'It's nothing,' she said.

'You hungry?' he said. 'I could buy you lunch or dinner or something.'

'I don't have time right now,' she said. 'I have to go to work. But you and your dog could walk me there if you want.'

'I'd like that,' he said and stood up. He walked to a closet and got his coat. The girl put on her coat, hat, and gloves and they walked out into the yard. It was dark as they went down Seventh Street towards the casinos and the downtown lights. Dan Mahony couldn't take control of her, she thought to herself, he could barely take control of himself. So as she walked, she felt all right with him there. Her hand fell next to his and she took it in hers and held it.

It was in a white envelope and addressed to her at the apartment. Postmarked Las Vegas. It was Jimmy Bodie's writing on it and her heart fell when she saw that it was. She sat outside her apartment on the sidewalk and opened it. The handwriting was shaky and the paper was lined and taken from a binder. It was written in pencil and much of it had been erased and rewritten.

Allison,

I hope you got my last letter. Your mom said she sent it but I don't know if she really did or if you got it. Anyway I guess you know that I know you are in Reno. Now I know where. It wasn't that hard to find out. I'm pretty certain I'm coming up. I wanted to let you know that I'm really moving to Montana or somewhere up there so I'll be passing your way. Vegas is too much. I thought I could live here but I can't. It's still a cesspool and it's getting worse by the day. I've finally straightened myself out. This time for good. I'm drawing that line North like I said. I always do what I say. I might move to Washingon, I don't know. You can make a ton of money up there. I'm a good mechanic so it shouldn't be that hard. I got a new girlfriend, she doesn't drink like you, and she's really good looking. She's gonna meet up with me when I get settled. Even so I want to see you. Maybe I'll stay in Reno, I don't know. Give me your phone number if you got one. Hope you're alive and doing all right.

Are you passing out everywhere? Still don't know why you just up and abandoned me. I know we went through some rough times but you're as much to blame as me. Anyway I apologized for my part. Even though I got this new gal, I still think about you all the time. At least mail me back. Call me collect if you want,

   Sincerely,
   Jimmy

A LATE NIGHT CONVERSATION

That night there was a fight in the parking lot of her apartment building. It was nighttime and her day off. She was watching TV. She had a frozen dinner in the oven. The fight was between two men and they yelled at each other and then suddenly they were fist fighting. She could hear one of the men screaming. She turned off the TV and the lights in the room and listened. There were times of silence, then it would start again. She moved a window shade to the side and looked out at two middle aged men wrestling on the pavement.

The apartment manager appeared and yelled at the two men, but they didn't stop. One of the men grabbed the other man by the hair and beat his head into the frozen parking lot. The apartment manager threatened to call the police and then after a while the police did come, and then an ambulance too.

She watched until the ambulance drove off and then turned the TV back on and ate her dinner by the light of it. That night she woke from a nightmare in which the new parents of her baby had left the boy alone in an alley. It was snowing out and they were walking down the road and then they set the baby boy next to a parked car and disappeared.

She woke in tears in a fit of anxiety that wouldn't end. She waited and waited for it to pass and when it didn't she bit down on the inside of her cheeks and with her hands she pinched her legs hoping it would calm her. She began crying. She went down a list of triggers to try and calm her nerves.

'Try to breathe,' he said suddenly to her.

'Why did I do it? Why did I give him away?'

''Cause your boyfriend's an asshole,' he said as he sat behind a large oak desk. His feet were set up and he was leaning back in his chair drinking a can of Budweiser. 'I'd bet he is one of the biggest dipshits I ever met in my life. He'd of made your life hell. He still could, I'm afraid.'

'Do you think he'll come here?'

'Well, he could. He might be serious about this new broad he's got, but it would be hard to pass up on you.'

'I'm a horrible person. That's why he'll come here. He'll find out about the baby, too. I deserve that."

'You aren't that horrible. Old scarface likes you. And you know what? I like him, too. He seems all right to me. He seems like a good guy for you. He reminds me a lot of myself, except for the scar and the no money and the job as a janitor. I ain't ever liked working a straight job.'

'Don't call him scarface.'

'You just like that he has a dog.'

'I like the dog, but I like him too,' she said.

'I wish I had a pitcher of iced tea. A man can only drink so many Budweisers.'

'I could make you some,' the girl said.

'No, you just sit there and relax. We're talking, after all.'

'I wish I didn't give him up. I wish it more than anything.'

'You did what you thought was right. If Jimmy knew you'd had a kid, you'd be right back there with him. And let me tell you, that would be rough. You think your dad was a son of a bitch? Jesus,

Jimmy would rival his own, I bet. Imagine being stuck with him for the rest of your life. Imagine him yelling at you and changing rules on you for forty years. I'd rather be in jail eating fifty eggs.'

'I helped burn down that house. I deserve what I get.'

'It never stops with you. Look, that wasn't the best move I've seen you make. Neither were those tattoos. I can't believe you'd put signs like that on you. I got to say I was pretty ashamed of you for that one. But that's what being weak gets you. You're gonna have to live with that. People do their worst when they're weak. You're no different. But now it's up to you to make your own way. Anyway, the past is the past. I mean, how many people did I send to die in *Road To Perdition*? I even tried to kill old Tom Hanks. I ain't a saint. My son in that one sure was a cocksucker. Jimmy and him, they're the same sort of man. They'll drag you down through it, kid. So you better stay clear of that shit heel.'

'Is it all right if I don't tell anyone I had him? Is it all right if I keep it to myself?'

'You've told me. If you want to tell someone, tell them. If you don't, don't. Remember me in *Somebody Up There Likes Me*?'

'Of course I do. You were a boxer.'

'I was probably the greatest boxer of all time. Anyway, I fought like hell in that one. I fought to get through, and Jesus it was tough but I got through. You saw how I ended up. You could do the same.'

'But I gave him away.'

'Look, I'll look in on the little tyke every day or so. I did a check on the family. If only I could've had them as my folks.'

'Can you check on Evelyn, too?'

'What the hell's she doing down in Mexico?'

'I don't know.'

'I'll see what I can do. But I'm afraid she's gonna go through some rough times too. That Junior, I'd like to put him on a chain gang and then send him down in the hole for a couple months. Maybe put him next to Hud. Hud, now that was a son of a bitch. I should have gotten millions for that part. Jesus, I could be mean.'

'What's gonna happen to Evelyn?'

'She's young. She'll be all right, but if she wants to come back, buy her a ticket. If you have to go down there and get her, get her.'

'All right.'

'So what else is going on?'

'Well, I really liked your girlfriend in *Fort Apache The Bronx*. I know I tell you that every time I see you, but it's true. It really is. I just wish she didn't die. She was my favorite girlfriend you ever had. I also liked the nurse you had when you're an old man in *Where The Money Is*. When she helps you break out and you get away with the armored truck heist and make off with the money and move to Europe. I think of you and me in that one.'

'I had them write that part for you.'

'I bet.'

'I did. Anyway, I sure wish you'd have brought us dinner. How's your fried chicken?'

'I could learn.'

'I'm glad you're taking your GED course. I think you should try college.'

'Jesus, you're aiming a bit high.'

'No, I'm not. Anyway, I hear you talking. I hear you wanting to give it a try.'

'I'm sure glad you're here.'

'You just watch yourself, kid, I'll always be here. And lay off the booze. You ain't much of a drunk. Remember *The Helen Morgan Story*? I admit I wasn't much in that one, but then you can't always pick your roles. Anyway, that poor gal Helen, she sure had a battle with the bottle. She went through and over and under the wringer in that one. I hate to say it but you could end up like that yourself if you don't keep a lid on it. So take my advice and stay off the booze, go to school, and most of all keep on the lookout for Jimmy. Him and his damn Northline. Remember, kid, there ain't no place where you can escape to. There's no place where there aren't weirdos and death and violence and change and new people. You head up to Wyoming or Montana and you'll run into the same things as you do in Vegas or New Orleans. You'll run into yourself.'

'Do you think he'll really show up?'

'He could. I'm not saying he will, but he sure could. But maybe that's the sorta test you need.'

'I don't feel like I could pass any test.'

'You'll be all right. We just have to toughen you up as much as we can. And save your dough and move to a nicer place. I don't like this neighborhood much. That fight tonight didn't set too well with me. Those two, let's hope they get evicted. And watch out for old bent back in 213. He's a pervert. And keep scarface around, you make him happier than he's been for a long time. And my gut says he's all right. If only he was as good looking as me. Anyway, kid, for fuck sakes lighten up on yourself.'

'I'll try.'

'I know you will, Ace.'

CAMPING

The dog sat in between them in the old pick-up. The sun was out and the day was warm as they headed towards Gerlach, Nevada, and the Black Rock Desert which lay beside the small desert town.

Allison was wearing sunglasses, her hair back in a pony tail, and she was talking and petting the dog.

'I've never really been camping.'

'We'll just sleep in the back of the truck,' Dan Mahony said. 'We can pretty much drive out onto the desert and camp wherever we want. It's beautiful at night with the stars. You can hear the trains roll by. It's so big and flat out on the playa, where we'll be, that they have the land speed records there. It goes on for miles and miles.'

'I made us fried chicken,' she said. 'Do you like fried chicken?'

'If you made it, I'll like it.'

'I bet,' she said.

He reached over and squeezed her hand.

'Can we have a fire?'

'I brought wood. It's gonna be cold as a mother out there tonight. In the morning we can go to a hot springs I know.'

'I didn't bring a swim suit,' she said.

'There will be no one out there most likely. You can just go in your underwear or we can go naked if you want.'

She moved closer to the dog and put her arm around him and the dog licked her arm.

'I made up my mind,' Dan said and looked at her.

'Made up your mind about what?'

'I'm gonna go back on as a plumber. At least part time. I'll sorta miss those guys at the VA, but the money's good with my uncle, and maybe it's time.'

'You should try if you want to, and if it doesn't work out I'm sure they'd let you come back to the hospital.'

'Probably,' he said.

'But remember, if it's too much don't do it. I like you just the way you are.'

'I know,' he said. 'That's what makes me want to try.'

It was nighttime and they lay naked in the bed of the truck under blankets and an old sleeping bag. The dog lay on Allison's feet as they both looked up at the stars.

'I don't feel so bad about myself being out here, looking at the stars this way,' she said.

'If I was as good looking as you, I'd feel pretty damn good.'

'I bet,' she said.

'It's true,' he said and took her hand in his.

'Do you think we'll hear the coyotes?'

'I hope so.'

'Maybe we could stay out here one more night.'

'I could if you want.'

'I don't want to go back there.'

'Me neither,' he said. 'Not just yet.'

The next morning she woke to the sound of Dan cooking breakfast. He had a fire going and she could smell the coffee and bacon he had cooking. The dog lay next to her. The sky was blue and gold and the sun had just started to rise over the mountains. She stayed like that for a long while, just listening to the fire.

When she sat up she petted the dog and said, 'Is it cold out there? You cold?'

'It's not so bad once you get out. But there's no need for you to get up. You stay in bed as long as you want.'

'I will then,' she said and smiled. 'It sure is beautiful out here.'

'When I got out of the hospital, when I was good enough to walk around, my uncle and I came out here. He's got a small camping trailer. It was fall and colder than shit but we stayed out here a week. During the day we'd just drive around. We'd explore, get firewood, go drinking at the bars in Gerlach. We'd drive up to Cedarville and Eagleville. We'd sit in the hot springs. Then in the evening just before dark we'd cook dinner, then we'd get in the trailer and try not to freeze to death. I was pretty damn down. I moped around an awful lot, and my uncle he didn't know what the hell to do with me. But by the end of the trip I was a hell of a lot better than I was when I first got in his truck on the way out here. Everything makes better sense when you're in the middle of nowhere.'

'Were you scared? After you drove home and it was over and your uncle left you at your place, did it all come back? The horrible feelings?'

'They did,' he said. 'But then I had this place to daydream in.'

'And they got less with time?'

'They can hijack you sometimes. But not like they used to. Not with you around. They don't seem as bad now. You want a cup of coffee?'

'No,' she said. 'I just want you to come back to bed. I'm starting to get cold.'

She had made a pot of coffee and put it in a Thermos. It was mid-morning and she was dressed in her warmest clothes, walking to the Cal Neva Casino where Dan Mahony sat on the sidewalk waiting for her.

'You must be tired,' he said. 'This is when you usually sleep, isn't it?'

'Yeah. I had a little trouble getting going but I wanted to come,' she said.

'I brought you some donuts.'

'You're gonna make me as fat as a cow,' she said. She sat next to him on the curb, and poured him a cup of coffee, opened the bag, and took one of the donuts.

'Can you hear it? They're just starting,' he said finally. He stood and helped her to her feet and together they walked down Center Street. He led her across Second Street and turned left towards Virginia.

There were policemen along Virginia Street and barriers closed it off. They waited until the cops let them cross, then they stood on the other side of the street amongst hundreds of people and watched as they got ready to tear down Harold's Club and the Nevada Club.

Dan took pictures of the buildings and of the workmen and trucks lined along Virginia Street. 'You know,' he said, 'Harold's Club was one of the first real casinos in this state. With the gimmicks and tricks, with the different kinds of games. Food specials and things like that. Harold Smith was the guy who ran it, then I think his kid ran it. Then I think his grandson, I'm not sure. But those guys ran it for years. In a way they started it all. And now it's gone. All the old places from that era are disappearing. I guess nothing stays the same. My uncle always says it seems like they just build strip malls now and tear down the beautiful brick buildings and landmarks that tell you about the things that have gone on here in the past. I guess no one here really cares about the past anymore. Might not seem like anything, but maybe it is. So many people move here and to Vegas and all over the West. They don't have any sorta roots. Maybe chain places are the only roots people have anymore. Maybe roots are Kentucky Fried Chicken and Taco Bell and Wendys. And places like Wal-Mart and K-Mart. The people moving here, they don't know what it was like before, and most of them probably don't care. Most people think this is an ugly town. I mean, that Harold's Club sign and the Nevada Club sign, they're beautiful to me. I don't know, but I really think they are.'

She took his hand and said, 'I guess people just need a place to live. Everyone does. It's hard when something you know changes, when things get worse or different and you remember when times were easier or at least felt safer and not so busy. That's what Las Vegas was like for me. Where everything changed, and changed for the worse.'

Dan looked across the street at the buildings. 'I remember my uncle and me walking down the strip and we'd stare at the Harold's Club sign and my uncle would ask me to tell him about all the people in it. Every time we'd pass by he'd do it. He'd ask me the name of the mountain man, and he'd ask me where the

Indian lived and if he was married, and how many kids the lady in the wagon train had. Sometimes we'd go eat at the Kilroy Diner inside the Nevada Club. Just my uncle and me. We'd sit across from each other and talk. He has this way about him that you can talk about anything with him. We'd just sit there and eat, sometimes he'd let me play Keno and sometimes he'd walk me through the casino and he'd tell me what a bunch of suckers all the folks there were. Maybe that's why I'm here right now, too. Scared to lose the memory of that. Of walking down this street with him staring at those old signs.'

A siren sounded and minutes later the buildings began to implode. They could hear as the charges began and suddenly the two buildings collapsed into rubble. In less than a minute it was over. There was dust and broken concrete and metal. The crowd of people stood, watching, some cheering. The girl looked around at them and then for an instant saw a man who, from the back, looked like Jimmy Bodie. His hair was the same, greased and black. The coat the man wore was black leather and looked like the one Jimmy had. Her heart froze in panic and she stood still, unable to move. Then the man turned, and she saw that it wasn't him.

She closed her eyes and said to herself, 'Please don't let him find me. Please, please, please, please.' She repeated it again and again until Dan spoke to her and she opened her eyes to see him. She grabbed his hand and kissed him. She kissed him with desperation. She kissed him with fear and hope and uncertainty. And in weakness she gave everything to him right then and there among the people and the fallen, ruined old casino buildings.